Praise for
GOD IN PINK

"If reading from the context of queer lit, what's most revolutionary about *God in Pink* is its insistence on faith ... *God in Pink* gives voice to the often voiceless, offer the outside world a window into their lives, and provide a glimmer of hope for change."
—*The Globe and Mail*

"One can only hope that a courageous and talented voice like Namir's can hold a mirror up to Iraqi citizens so they can at least start seeing their fellow gay and lesbian citizens as valued human beings and not evil sinners to be ostracized, oppressed, silenced, and murdered."
—*Bay Area Reporter*

"This book should be on everyone's shelf—religious and non-religious alike. It is a raw, passionate, gritty tale of not only these two men who chose different paths, and are still making choices, but also of the many people around them who make their own life decisions to love, hate, accept, kill, tolerate or repel them."
—*Philadelphia Gay News*

GOD IN PINK
Copyright © 2015 by Hasan Namir

SECOND PRINTING: 2016

ARSENAL PULP PRESS
Suite 202 – 211 East Georgia St.
Vancouver, BC V6A 1Z6
Canada
arsenalpulp.com

The publisher gratefully acknowledges the support of the Canada Council for the Arts and the British Columbia Arts Council for its publishing program, and the Government of Canada (through the Canada Book Fund) and the Government of British Columbia (through the Book Publishing Tax Credit Program) for its publishing activities.

Canadä

Cover design by Gerilee McBride
Interior design by Oliver McPartlin
Edited by Linda Field, Brian Lam, and Susan Safyan

Printed and bound in Canada

Library and Archives Canada Cataloguing in Publication

Namir, Hasan, 1987-, author
God in pink / Hasan Namir.

Issued in print and electronic formats.
ISBN 978-1-55152-606-5 (paperback).—ISBN 978-1-55152-607-2 (epub)

I. Title.

PS8627.A536G64 2015   C813'.6   C2015-903481-7
                                                C2015-903482-5

GOD
IN
PINK

a novel

HASAN
NAMIR

ARSENAL PULP PRESS   VANCOUVER

*"In the Name of God, the Most Beneficent,
the Most Merciful …"*

Forgive me. I don't know your name. After all, I have only seen you once. I hope you are able to help me since I have no one else to reach out to. I know you must be wondering why, out of all people, I chose you. I don't have the answer myself. But I can tell you this ... when I looked into your eyes, I thought you were somewhat different.

Now, I will begin my story.

Do you really know our city, Baghdad, sir? Most people would try to find eloquent words to describe it. For me, Baghdad is a city that has evaporated into tiny particles of filth. We often think that our lives are ordinary. We often look down on the streets, crowded with our fathers going to work, our children going to school, and our mothers praying for our souls and taking care of our homes. Some say that Baghdad has changed since the war, but I believe that things are the same. We are the same. I'm the same. Our Muslim brothers are the same. Everyone sees "justice" differently.

My parents are both dead. My mother passed away when I was born, leaving my father to raise my brother and me. Then my father was executed; his only crime being that he wanted to practice religious freedom.

Mohammed is a professor of English at Baghdad University. He says that having obtained his PhD from the University of Oxford in England is the greatest source of pride in his life. As a professor, he earns enough money for our family, which means that once every two weeks, he can bring home one or two kilos of meat. My brother is happy with his life as long as we are too. To him, happiness doesn't mean a brand-new car or luxurious food, it means a stable life.

My brother met his wife Noor in England; theirs was a

love story that blossomed for years. Their love was strong; they waited patiently, only marrying after their return to Iraq. My brother and his wife cannot conceive a child, and for them adoption is not an option. My brother explained that in Islam, it is *haram* to adopt children. Is this true, sir? I wonder.

Mohammed has always taken care of me and been a father figure to me, helping to raise me when our father was fighting for the rights of Shiites. Our father often travelled to the city of Karbala, where he would participate in private Shiite ceremonies. During his reign, Saddam forbade any Shiite activities. One day, on the Day of Ashura, years ago, our father and many of his Shiite friends commemorated the martyrdom of Imam Husayn Ibn Ali, the grandson of Prophet Muhammad in Karbala. That day, Saddam had laid down orders for the arrest of our father and many of his friends. They were all eventually executed, my father's blood flowing at the feet of Saddam. As for my mother, I don't have any memory of her; she died during my birth. All I have of her is a single black and white photograph.

Do you ever feel like a prisoner in your own room? I often lie on my bed looking up at the ceiling and wishing I were dead. Or perhaps that I could move to a different country far less religious than Iraq and more open to personal freedom. I don't want to feel this way. But I know what I am. Nothing can change that.

Many times I have thought of escaping, but where would I go? What place would accept me for who I am? As beautiful as Baghdad is, her people are still closed-minded and repressive.

I've not shared my secret with anyone. If my brother found out, he'd kill me.

One day, consumed by sadness and confusing thoughts,

I wanted desperately to talk to someone about my feelings. But who? As I sat at my desk trying to make sense of life, trying to understand my purpose, there was a knock at the door.

"Come in," I said. It was Mohammed, a warm smile on his face.

"How are you doing today?"

"Fine," I said vaguely.

"Any exams coming up?"

"No."

He asked if there was something wrong.

"No. Why?"

"I'm just asking."

All of a sudden, I felt overwhelmed and quickly wiped the tears from my eyes, forcing a smile. It's just how things went in this house.

"Are you crying?" he asked.

I shook my head. Mohammed sat on the bed and looked at me, waiting for a response. I turned away.

"Look at me," he whispered.

I sighed. "I told you, everything is all right."

He stood up to leave, but on his way out, said, "Remember, I'm always here for you."

I guess I was supposed to believe that, but if he knew the truth, it would be a different story.

Later, after praying, I passed Mohammed on the staircase.

"Where are you going?" he asked.

"Out with friends."

"Why?"

"Why not?"

"Do you not have exams?"

"I told you I don't."

My brother checked his watch. "It's already eleven. When will you be back?"

Wanting to get away, I said, "I'm not a kid anymore. Did you forget I'm twenty years old?"

"I've not forgotten. But I'm worried about you."

I stared at my older brother for a moment, my only family. But I didn't want to listen to him.

"I'll be back soon, I promise," I said, and hurried down the stairs.

Outside the house, standing for a second, my back against the door and eyes closed, I inhaled the warm polluted air. It was good to have escaped my brother's interrogation.

I started to walk toward the main road and hailed a taxi, hesitating at first when the driver asked where I wanted to go. I was embarrassed to tell him.

"Can you take me to shaar'a Karada, please?"

I asked him to drop me off a street away from my destination. The cabbie stopped on Karada Street and looked at me quizzically, but didn't say anything. I quickly paid him and walked away.

Two blocks later I arrived at my destination, a private club. Entering, I spotted a familiar face. He was waiting for me.

In my second year at university, I was always the quiet one, never speaking up during class. One day, the professor gave us a group assignment; I was paired up with this boy, Ali. Unlike me, Ali had a charming personality and was always outspoken. He invited me over to his house after school to work on the assignment. I thought about asking him to my house instead, and then realized that probably wasn't a good idea. My brother and his wife, well ...

So, I agreed to go to Ali's.

As he drove me to his house, Ali did most of the talking. I spoke only when Ali asked a question. He gave me a brief introduction to his life: he lived with his parents, but they were never around. His father was a diplomat and his parents frequently travelled all over the world. Ali said he wanted to start a business after graduating, but he wasn't sure what kind.

"How often do you see your parents?"

"Not that often, really. Once or twice a year. I often think of them and miss them a lot."

I began to feel connected to Ali. He missed his parents like I missed my mother. At least Ali's parents were still alive, but if they were never around, what was the difference?

Ali's house was luxurious, the size of a villa. Two guards opened the gates as he drove into the compound. I was in awe as we passed an enormous water fountain and parked across from the main door. Ali took me on a tour of the seemingly endless gardens, where I could smell the lemony aroma of the gardenias. Inside, he showed me the majestic living room filled with antiquities. I was stunned; he lived in what looked to me like a Mesopotamian palace.

Ensconced in his bedroom, we worked on the assignment together, though my mind was anywhere but on school work. When he wasn't looking, I stared at Ali's green eyes, his face that glowed like the blazing sun. I felt myself sinking into a deep pool.

Ali turned to me and smiled. "Forget about this. Let's have a drink."

"Oh, I ... I don't drink."

"Come on, one drink won't hurt." I had always been curious about alcohol, and saying no to Ali would be considered rude. One drink couldn't hurt.

We sat in the living room eating *baba ghanouj* and drinking *arak*. My brother never allowed alcohol in the house. At first, I hated the strong bitter taste, but after the first drink, I wanted more. Before long, we were both drunk; I passed out on the couch.

Later, when I woke up and checked my watch, I was shocked that it was so late. Ali was at the other end of the couch, asleep himself.

"I need to go home," I said, waking him.

He rubbed his eyes. "You can stay over for the night."

"I can't. My brother will kill me."

"I don't see what the big deal is. Keep me company."

"I know, but my brother—"

"Fine. I'll give you a ride home."

And so ended our first night together.

We didn't speak of it until one day the following week, after a class, when Ali and I left the campus and went for a drive. We stopped outside Zawraa Park, where we went for a walk past the amusement rides, through the blossoming flowers, and into the woods. It was secluded and isolated. We looked at each other.

"Are you ..." Ali said, his voice trailing off.

"Kiss me, Ali," I whispered boldly. He pulled me in for a rough kiss; we breathed in each other's warm bodies. Suddenly he turned me around and pulled my jeans down to my feet. He wet his fingers with his spit and ... I shut my eyes, letting him in. I had fantasized about my first encounter with Ali, and now ...

At the club, I pulled Ali's head toward mine and kissed him passionately before dragging him to the dance floor. I had never felt so free in my life. Later we took a break to have a drink at the bar with our friend Bashar. Ali told us both, "I have a surprise for you. This weekend, I'm having a costume party. It will be fun!" A costume party? I was immediately hesitant, not sure what to wear. But Ali seemed so enthusiastic, so I was game, and so was Bashar.

Later, Ali and I went back to Zawraa Park. Under a moon that shone down upon us from between the purple clouds, we took off our shoes and, holding hands, stepped into the waters of the lake. No one else was there.

"Beautiful, isn't it?" Ali said, looking around.

"You're beautiful," I replied, smiling. "I love you." Letting go of Ali's hand for a second, I looked up at the sky, imploring, "Do you hear me, Allah?"

At the edge of the lake, we sat on the sand, water lapping at our feet. It felt as though nothing in the world could stop us.

When Ali dropped me off at home, I kissed him good-night and climbed out of the car. I looked up and saw Noor staring at us from the window. Did she see the kiss?

I was in my room and about to undress when there was a knock at the door.

"Come in."

"Where were you?" Noor looked at me suspiciously.

"Sorry. I was at a friend's house."

"Your brother was worried about you all night, until I made him go to bed. You know he has to work in the morning."

"Again, I'm sorry—"

"Who is he?"

"Who?"

"The man you were with."

"He's just a friend."

She stared at me coldly.

"Are you all right?" I asked.

"Who is he?" she repeated.

"I told you, he's a friend. What do you mean?"

"Tell me the truth."

I couldn't.

It was something I couldn't control or change, even if I wanted to. But would my brother, my sister-in-law, or any other Muslim here accept it? Would you accept it, Sheikh? I didn't have to think about it for a second. No, these people were raised to listen to the word of God. If He says that homosexuality is a sin and that gays need to be severely punished, then Muslims must obey Him and condemn us.

"What do you mean?" I asked again.

"Nothing," she said, turning to leave. She hesitated in the doorway, asking, "Is there something you want to tell me, *habibi*?"

"No," I replied curtly.

"You know you can talk to me any time."

"I know. Thanks."

I still wasn't sure if she'd seen Ali and me kiss, but I was grateful for her kindness.

It was the night of Ali's costume party. I had decided not to put on my costume until I arrived at Ali's house. He gave me a hand, helping me with my makeup. When I was done, I looked in the mirror and smiled. It wasn't me there. Instead, there was a beautiful, fully made-up woman with blonde hair.

"Oh my god," I said. "I look like Sailor Moon."

"You look sexy," Ali said, grinning as he leaned over and kissed me. He was wearing a disco-era white suit, and together, we looked like an Iraqi Ken and Barbie.

Downstairs, we greeted the guests, including Bashar, who was dressed as a belly dancer. We danced and drank the night away. I know you might be offended, Sheikh, and I wouldn't be surprised if you stop reading here. But I hope that you will continue.

Later, I woke up in the middle of the night with a start. I was still at Ali's house. I checked my watch, and was shocked to have let time defeat me again. Trying to get up, I fell right back down—too much drink. I nudged Ali, waking him.

"What?"

"Can you give me a ride home?"

"Stay the night."

"No. My brother's probably still awake, waiting for me."

"Always your brother."

"Ali, you know my situation."

He soon fell back to sleep. I realized that he was too drunk to drive, so I took a taxi home. But not before I'd removed the makeup, transforming back to my old self.

At home, just as I'd suspected, Mohammed was wide awake, waiting in the living room.

"Where were you?" There was anger in his voice.

"Out. With friends."

He stared at me, scrutinizing me from top to bottom. "What's this?" He pointed at my face. My heart stopped.

"What?"

He stood up and put a finger to the side of my mouth, then held it in front of me. "This."

There was a red smudge on his finger.

Shit, I thought. "Nothing. I'm very tired, Mohammed. I need to go to sleep."

"Is there something you want to tell me?"

"No. Good night."

"Are you seeing someone?"

"What?"

"What's her name?"

"None of your business."

He smiled, happy now. Maybe this was what he'd wanted to hear all along. Maybe it was what he needed to hear.

The next night at the club, Ali, Bashar, and I sat at a table as Arabian pop music played over the speakers. We were talking about nothing in particular when Bashar suddenly blurted out, "I'm thinking of leaving the city."

"What? Where would you go?" I asked.

"Anywhere. As long as it's far away from Iraq."

"Why?"

"My father found out about me." Ali and I exchanged looks.

"Are you okay?" Ali asked.

"No." Bashar took a big sip from his drink. "I just can't live here anymore."

"You can come to live at my house," Ali offered.

"Thanks, but I'm staying with Khaled," Bashar said, referring to his boyfriend. "He's going to get me out of here, out of this shitty country."

Suddenly there was a commotion at the entrance. Two masked and armed men rushed in. The three of us stood up as others in the club rushed toward the doors in a panic, fearing that they would be shot. But the masked men pushed their way in our direction until they were face to face with Bashar. Before Ali and I could react, they opened fire and shot him repeatedly. He fell to the floor, dead.

The killers left as quickly as they had arrived. We were in shock; it felt like we were watching a movie. Blood poured from Bashar's wounds—the life of this beautiful human, our friend, had ended so quickly, so suddenly. We sat on the floor next to him, sobbing, but no one dared to call the police because if any of us had, we would all have been put in prison for being at a gathering of homosexuals.

I knew this was a targeted killing, that our dear friend had lost his life because his family, his society, couldn't accept him. Ali and I left the club in shock and tears.

The next day, we had a private gathering at Ali's house to honour and remember Bashar. His killers, of course, would not be brought to justice. It was as if he had never existed. I prayed for divine justice.

Back home that night, we ate in silence at the dinner table. I looked at Mohammed and thought: Really? Are you always there for me? If you knew about me, would you kill me in front of the neighbours, would you mourn if I were killed like Bashar? I realized that my brother wasn't to blame. I was a coward because I didn't have the nerve to speak to my brother, to try to explain. I told myself that I should be braver.

After dinner, I went to my room and was reading a book when Mohammed entered without knocking.

"Are you planning to see that girl again?" he asked.

"There is no girl," I said.

"That's what I thought." He paused. What now, I wondered. "I found you a wife."

"What?"

"I want to make Mama and Baba happy in their graves. They wanted grandchildren. I promised them that." I didn't know what to say.

"I know it's a lot to take in, so I'll leave you now to think about it."

A short time later, I heard my brother and sister-in-law whispering. I went to the door to listen.

"Are you sure?" she asked.

"He didn't say anything, but I assure you he's going to accept the offer."

"What if he doesn't?"

"He doesn't really have a choice here." Leaning my forehead against the door, I listened intently.

"Give him some time. I'm sure he will find someone. The boy just needs time."

"No. Time is running out."

This moment had come a lot earlier in my life than I'd expected.

Later that night, I left the house after making sure the family was asleep and took a taxi to the club to meet Ali. I don't know why I was shocked to see two armed police officers standing out front and a sign on the door saying, "Closed, *lawat.*" As I was about to leave, a hand grabbed my arm and pulled me to the side. It was Ali.

"What's going on?" I asked.

"Not here. Come with me." Silently, we walked to his car and got in.

"What happened?" I asked again.

"The fucking cops found out about the club and closed it down. Fuck them, fuck this country. I'm so fucking sick of this shit." He fell silent and we stared at each other, lost and speechless.

"I'm leaving," Ali said.

"What?"

"I'm leaving Iraq. Bashar was right."

When Ali saw the tears threatening to fill my eyes, he kissed my forehead, trying to comfort me. But now his touch felt like a stranger's.

"I can't live here anymore. It's not safe for me," he continued.

"Where are you going?"

"Turkey."

"You can't," I pleaded. "Please don't leave me here alone." I felt like a small child about to lose his parents again.

"I'd never leave you here. Never," he said, surprise in his voice. "You'll come with me."

"But ... I can't leave my family. I don't want to hurt them."

"Sooner or later, they'll find out who you are, and they'll either disown you or kill you ..."

"But—"

"We can't let them slaughter us like animals. We deserve a better life."

"Yes, but—"

"Go get your stuff. You're going to stay with me for a few days until we can leave."

"Tonight?"

"Do you want to come with me or not?"

That night, at home, I sat at my desk, struggling to write a letter to my brother. It took me hours. I had to stop every once in a while and start over. But then I changed my mind and scrapped it entirely. Even through written words, I was afraid of confronting him. Determined, I packed my suitcase quickly. Everything was ready.

I felt like I could trust Ali. I didn't know how on God's earth I would get into Turkey without a visa, but I put my full faith in the man I loved and in God. When I knew that Mohammed and Noor were asleep, I left the house quietly with my suitcase. Ali was waiting outside.

Hesitating, I thought of the sorrow that I knew Mohammed and Noor would feel when they awoke and discovered I was gone. I imagined my parents and how they might have felt. Then an image appeared in front of me: my head severed from my body, a sign placed on it with the word "*lotee*." That is what they call us. *Lotee*. I imagined people spitting on me, calling me names, and I imagined sitting across from you, Sheikh, listening to you. I thought about living the rest of my life in an unknown land with a man I truly loved. I felt glued to the spot.

"Ali ..."

"Come on, man. Let's go," Ali commanded, spurring me to action.

We got into his car. He put on an Amr Diab CD and started to drive away. But then I looked back at the house and thought of my family. My determination was melting away quickly. "Ali, I can't go with you," I said.

He stopped the car in the middle of the street.

"Ali, what are you doing?" I asked, but he didn't say anything. Behind us, angry drivers began to honk their horns.

He didn't seem particularly upset or surprised. In fact, there was a calm look on his face. Finally, he turned, smiled at me, and said, "I didn't think you'd be brave enough."

"Ali ..." I reached toward him.

Then, in one fast motion, he pulled a gun from his pocket, aimed it at the side of his head, and pulled the trigger. Blood sprayed everywhere, including on me. In shock, hardly knowing what I was doing, I jumped out of the car and ran away. I left him there as the cars behind Ali's continued to sound their horns. It was cowardly, Sheikh, but I was terrified and stunned.

Now I wonder if, all along, this is what "Turkey" meant to

him. And here I am, a young man stuck inside four walls in my brother's house. I am to marry a woman whom I have never met. How will she live with a homosexual? Then again, she might never know. We could live our entire lives together and be blessed with children. But I am sure that we would be miserable. Is that the kind of the life I desire? Should I just end it like Ali did? What about my hopes? Could I even allow myself to dream of becoming someone? I struggle every day with my decision to abandon Ali. If I had said yes, would we have been able to find a place that welcomed us? Does Allah even love us? I have read the Qur'an twice already, and it feels like, in Islam, God does not love us. But why, then, did He create us?

I am writing to you for answers. I need your help. Are you willing to help me? You do not know my name; you do not know where I live. To you, I am just a young man who loved another man and realized that he cannot be the person that his family wants him to be. And he needs your help. I need your help. I am writing to you because, even though I have seen you just once, I know you are someone who can help me.

There is only one way that you can tell me that you will help me. I will come and see you again, along with the many men and women who go every Friday to listen to your wise counsel in the mosque. I ask you now to talk about homosexuality next Friday—and condemn it. Please. Condemn it. But if you mention one word, then I'll know you want to help me. One word. And when you say that word, I will come to you so that you can help me see the light. I need some guidance. I need someone. I do not want to meet the same grotesque end as Bashar and Ali.

One word…

Pink.

Praise be to Allah. I place the letter down and check the clock on my night table: 1:30. In four hours, I have to wake for the morning prayers. Yet I cannot keep my eyes closed for a single minute. *Ya Allah*. I turn my head and gaze at Shams, my wife, before getting up for a drink of water. Who is this young man? He knows me. But I certainly don't know him at all. I wonder why he has chosen to write to me, of all people. He didn't hold back any details in his letter, and that frightens me. Why the colour *werdy*? Is it metaphorical? I sit at the table and wonder, who is this man? What if he is a friend disguised as someone else? Oh, *astaghfirul-lah*—Allah forbids. I don't want to have to suffer, knowing that a friend is ... Allah forbids. Saying the word would bring sin to me and my family.

I go to the living room and open the Qur'an and begin to read. Allah forgive me. I cannot concentrate and close the book. The letter writer wants me to speak out about a sinful matter in front of many men and women, even children. God forbid! Back in my room, I return to the Qur'an and try to forget about the letter.

Tick ... tock ... The clock taunts me. I look around, am overwhelmed with thoughts. I lean over and lightly caress Shams as she sleeps. How would she feel about this? Then again, what is she dreaming of right now? It cannot be of that letter. How can Allah allow me to read such filth? I mean, if I met this man, I would hand him over to our Muslim brothers. *Allahu-Akbar*.

I grab the letter from the night table and go to the kitchen to fetch a box of matches. But with the match lit and the flame ready, it suddenly goes out in a puff of wind. I turn around and see the face of a small pink creature that I don't recognize.

"Now, why would you do that?" he asks.

My heart races as I quickly recite a Qur'anic verse. *Ya rab ehofthly ebny wa zawjty*. Please, God, protect them from any harm.

"Shh, you will wake your wife and son. Is that what you want?"

"No."

"Then, listen."

I slump into a chair and stare at the pink creature. He reminds me of a mythical cupid, with two tiny, fluttery butterfly wings. He flies close to the ceiling and smiles down at me. I close my eyes, hoping that I'm in a dream. But when I open them, the creature is still there.

"Who are you? What do you want from me?"

"I don't believe we've met before. You are Ammar—"

"How did you—"

"And I'm the Angel Gabriel."

I gaze up at him. "Angel Gabriel? I ... I don't believe it."

Gabriel begins to recite a verse from the Qur'an: "Anyone who opposes Gabriel should know that he has brought down this Qur'an into your heart, in accordance with God's will, confirming previous scriptures, and providing guidance and good news for the believers."

I clap my hands, sneering at the same time. "So you can memorize verses from the Qur'an. That's impressive."

"Hey, where did your beard go?"

I touch my face and, to my horror, my beard is gone. "What? What did you do with it, you little monster?" How will the faithful at the mosque take me seriously without a beard? What's worse, the creature now laughs at me like the *shaitan* laughing at Allah.

"Okay, okay. I'm not a mean angel after all."

I touch my face again. My beard is back.

"Ammar, I hope this confirms for you who I am."

"I still don't believe this. *Astaghfirullah*."

"In any case, what were you going to do?"

"I was going to burn a letter. Is something wrong with that? Is it *haram*?"

"This man is seeking your help, and you turn him down. Is that what God expects from us?"

I remain defiantly silent.

"To be a sheikh isn't just to lecture and pray and read the Qur'an. You have to help those who are in need."

I look up at the angel. "But how can I help a homosexual man?" I ask.

The little creature falls silent, looking down in sadness. I realize that I am trapped inside a dream.

"Ammar ..."

"Yes, Gabriel."

"Help this man. He needs you."

Then suddenly Gabriel is gone and a pink blossom wafts down, as if from the heavens. I catch it before it can land. Holding it in my hands, I marvel at the beauty and perfection of Allah's work. I put the flower in a glass of water and sit back to admire its hypnotizing effect.

Inhaling deeply, I lay on my bed, but can't shut my eyes. The walls are closing in. I hold my breath. A force inside me wants to escape my body and scream loud enough that all of Iraq will hear. But who will listen? The sheikh? Mohammed or Noor? Or maybe Ali, whose soul continuously haunts me?

A knock on the door disturbs my thoughts. The door opens, and Mohammed enters with a smile on his face.

"Good morning." My sense of time is off. I had thought it was dark outside, but he opens my curtains and now I see that the sun is shining.

"Come on, Ramy, get up. I don't want to be late for class."

He leaves the room. I stare up at the ceiling where a shimmering light is reflected from the trees outside. I want to hide within them.

Later, I find myself in the passenger seat of Mohammed's car as he drives. I touch my forehead; it is wet. He looks at me and says, "Are you okay? Why are you sweating?"

"Am I?" I laugh nervously.

He doesn't pursue it. Instead, he turns on the radio. A song by Fayrouz, the Lebanese diva, is playing; she is known as "Ambassador to the Stars." Most Arabs listen to her in the morning; her melodic voice has a touch of melancholy.

Mohammed pulls a cigarette from his shirt pocket and lights up. I have the urge to ask for one, but before I can, he turns and offers me the pack. I look at him quizzically, then take one. It's as if Mohammed is a stranger. Lighting up, I inhale the smoke and let it out in a long sigh.

"I know something is wrong," he says. "But it's okay. I don't expect a response yet. Think about it and come talk to me when you're ready."

We don't speak for the rest of the trip. As I inhale again, I begin to feel calm, rejuvenated. Looking out the window, I see all around us the evidence of war: decaying buildings, fallen bricks, pot-holed streets. I stare in passing at what's left of the famous University of Baghdad. Oh, the beautiful destruction, the heart-warming death of an historical school. I have looked at pictures in old yearbooks from decades past and wish things had stayed the same. Last week, a bomb exploded near the college, destroying almost everything around it. Just another typical day. The fact that the school still exists is astonishing. It wasn't so long ago that students were taught by American and British professors, but now our Iraqi brothers pretend to be American and British and want to continue to teach the students in English. Their dream is to be as good as the Americans and the British. But such dreams are hopeless.

Before the war, students were from educated and upper-class families. Now, the University of Baghdad is like any other—it is no longer an elite institution. But Mohammed still takes his job seriously, still tries to maintain his sense of status.

After he parks the car, we part and I walk toward my classroom. Ali's presence seems to surround me all the time. He breathes when I breathe, he walks when I walk, he talks when I talk. If only I could go back in time; if only I'd made a different decision.

In class, the other students and I sit patiently at our desks, waiting for the professor. The clock ticks as I stare at Ali's empty seat beside me. I can see his sly smile, feel his arm brush against mine.

"Where is Professor Mahmood?" someone finally asks. I hear the question, but my mind is elsewhere. I am floating on a cloud with Ali, surrounded by blue sky and sunshine. But my solace is interrupted by a school official who has entered the room and is standing at the front of the class.

"Students, Professor Mahmood ..." He trails off and looks down at the podium. He doesn't have to tell us more. Professor Mahmood is just another victim. What makes him any different than the rest? One by one, they leave this country. Or worse. I always envied those who could get away.

That evening, I sit quietly at our table eating dinner with Mohammed and Noor, who has made *dolmas*, stuffed grape leaves with minced meat and rice.

"I got a call from Gamal today," she says, turning to me. "Do you remember Uncle Gamal, *habibi*?"

Uncle Gamal is Noor's older brother. He spent many years partying and living the wild single life. Noor once told me that every time the family brought it up, he refused to settle down. But eventually he married a Kurdish woman he met at work. Soon after marrying, though, they left the country.

"How's he doing?" I ask.

She sighs. "Not so good. Still trying." She falls silent and looks down at her plate. For the rest of the meal, Noor doesn't say another word. I wonder what has happened to him.

After dinner, Mohammed goes to the living room to watch television. In the kitchen, Noor is wiping the table.

"Here, I'll help you." I take over from Noor, who begins washing the dishes.

"So, you didn't finish your story at dinner," I say.

She rinses a dish and turns to glance at me. "You mean Gamal?"

"Yes. What happened to him?"

"You know why he left to go overseas, don't you?"

"No, not really. I just remember he and his wife left very suddenly."

"Well, they've been trying to have a child for some time now—" She falls silent again, sits down on a chair, and continues, "It's hard, you know." I can see her eyes are wet. I embrace her.

Bismillah. I'm sitting at the table. I can't recall whether or not I slept. My body aches. But I try to smile to brighten my son's morning. Jaffar is ten years old. I've followed in the family's footsteps and rejected institutionalized education for him. Like my father, I believe that the best education is through experience and the Qur'an and the teachings of the Prophet. Jaffar, now a young *imam*, accompanies me to the mosque every morning and listens to my lecture. When we arrive home, he reads the Qur'an with me; he performs the prayer ritual five times a day with me as well. One day, I hope that he will become a sheikh like me. I see in him a younger version of myself, wearing the white *dishdasha* and cap on his head. Of course, Jaffar doesn't yet have facial hair, but he will. *Masha'Allah.*

He finishes eating his *pache,* his favourite dish. My plate is still full. I prefer chicken, but I enjoy seeing Jaffar's face when he eats this meal, his eyes aglow. He looks up and says, "Should we go now, Baba?" I consult my watch and answer, "Not yet, we still have time, man." I like to call my son "man" because I want him to think he is one, even though he is still young. When I look at him, I see the grown man that he will become.

Shams comes toward us in her nightgown, smiling as she takes our plates and returns to the kitchen. I remember when I first met her. She had thick red hair and didn't cover it with a *hejab* then. She was beautiful. Her father and my father had been friends for years. I wanted to marry her, but it was against Sharia; she had to be properly covered before I could call her my wife. At first, she declined my proposal. After we were married, I told her that she could not eat at the same table as me. She said that when she was growing up, her family did not separate the men and women at meals, so it bothered her; I think it may still, but it is a tradition passed down from my great-great-grandfather. We accept it for what it is. I cannot break with tradition.

Jaffar grabs his bag, which contains a copy of the Qur'an and some notebooks. I taught him to write down anything that he finds important in my lectures. Then he memorizes the notes so that he will never forget them.

The two of us leave and walk toward the mosque, only a few blocks away from our house. We are close enough that I don't have to worry about a car, bicycle, or any other form of transportation. As we approach the mosque, the sun illuminates the oval silver-plated dome; we enter through the ceramic-decorated door, unlike the others. Removing my shoes, I hand them to Jaffar, who places them inside a cabinet. The faithful are already gathered, seated on the floor; when I clear my throat, all of them rise. I walk toward the wall in front of them and sit against it. There are still ten minutes until my lecture begins. But for the first time in a long time, I feel unprepared. I look at the ceiling, knowing that all eyes are on me.

This morning, I have not yet taken my place in what I call the king's chair. It is the same one that my father sat in before me and his father before that. But I feel unworthy and overwhelmed. Beads of sweat form on my forehead. What will I tell my people today? I look at the men looking back at me; in my mind, all of them are wearing *werdy*. Which one of them wrote the letter? Which one of them will reveal his identity? I glance at my watch, then finally stand up and make my way toward the king's chair. It is rather ordinary, yet to the other *Muslimeen* of the mosque, it has special significance. Only I am allowed to climb the five steps and sit upon it.

Looking out at a sea of silent, staring eyes, I feel unworthy. I cannot read them; I cannot differentiate between who is true and honourable and who is not.

Jaffar is the key to unlocking my mind and freeing it. I look at him and smile, then begin with my *salaams*. The worshippers return the *salaams* in loud voices. I debate whether or not to talk about the *lawats. La!*

"No!" a voice screams in my ear. I look around, trying to find the source.

"I am right here," it says. I turn to the right and see a woman dressed in a black burka. All the men fade away. The room is empty now, except for the woman and me.

"Who are you?" I ask.

"Don't you know me, Ammar?"

"Who are you?" I repeat.

She laughs, and the sound echoes throughout the mosque.

"I'm sorry. I don't know you."

"I am Abaddon. Don't you remember me?"

"No. I've never seen you before."

"Strange. I feel like I've known you my whole life."

"But ..." I look around. "Where did everyone go?"

"Does it really matter?"

"Why are you here? What do you want from me?"

"Homosexuality, is it now?"

I look at her in surprise. Turning away, I see two men kissing. I shut my eyes. Abaddon laughs.

"Do you see what I mean?" she asks. She comes close and touches my lips, caresses my beard.

I push her away, saying, "I'm a married man."

She backs away, smiles, and says, "Yes, you're a *rejjal*. Do you want everyone to think otherwise?"

"I don't know what you're talking about."

"All the rumours, all the gossip. Is it worth it?"

"No!"

"If you have any respect for God, then forget about it. You are not to give a lecture on homosexuality. It is wrong; it is forbidden." Then she is gone in a cloud of darkness.

A chill crawls down my spine. Cold and shivering, I see eyes staring, judging me, mocking, laughing. I stand up from the king's chair and stumble down the steps. Jaffar approaches me, saying something I don't understand. Someone hands me a glass of water. I struggle to breathe, feeling numb. As I shut my eyes, I hear one word echoing softly in my head ... *werdy*. Pink.

I sit at my desk, hard at work solving mathematics problems. But no one seems to be solving any of my problems. Mohammed enters my bedroom without knocking. Looking up, I think I can read a smile on his face. It involves a girl, no doubt.

"What's going on?" I ask, feigning innocence.

He hands me three photographs of young women, all of them wearing makeup and beauty-pageant smiles.

He sits down next to me. "What do you think?"

I look at the pictures. Nothing comes to mind.

"This one's name is Yassmine."

She is named after a beautiful flower. I suppose I must be her Aladdin, holding a magic lamp, fulfilling her wishes and mine. And we'll live happily ever after on a heavenly carpet ride. But if I had a magic lamp, I'd be soaring high in the sky, and when I fell, it would be into the arms of a man, not her.

"What do you think?" he persists.

I am thinking of another life, a different future, with someone else.

"She's nice."

He pauses, expecting more. But what else does he want to hear?

"That's it?"

I shrug.

"Do you like her?"

"It's just a picture."

He grins. "I figured that you'd say that. Noor and I can set up a date. We can all go out with her family, and you can meet her."

This is how people date in Iraq. The man and woman are both accompanied by their families, and they all meet together at a restaurant. The prospective couple can go off for a walk by themselves, but in the end, they will each leave with their respective families. This passes for courting here.

"What do you say?" Mohammed urges as he takes the photograph from me. "She comes from a good family. She's graduating soon."

"But I haven't graduated myself."

"Why is that important?"

"How am I going to feed her and our twenty children?" My sarcasm silences him. I look into his eyes and sense anger.

"Do you want this or not?"

I hesitate, thinking. Do I want to marry a woman and make children with her and then realize that I can't be with her anymore because I've fallen in love with a man?

"Answer me."

I sigh. "You never answered my question."

"What question?"

"How can I support my family when I'm still a student?"

He smiles and puts his hand on my shoulder. "Don't worry about that. I will take care of you."

My brother seems to have a solution for everything. That annoys me.

"I don't want to depend on you, Mohammed. I want to make it on my own."

"Get a job, then."

"Doing what?"

"You can be my assistant. I need someone to help me mark exams and assignments."

I feel myself frowning. I should have known that Mohammed would somehow link any job opportunity for me to him. It seems that whatever I do, wherever I go, I'll never get away.

Noor knocks on the door. "What are you two talking about?" she asks.

"I'm showing Ramy the photos," Mohammed says. "But he's not being very reasonable."

"Mohammed, let me talk with Ramy," she says. He gives the photos to Noor and leaves the room.

"Ramy, do you want to get married?" Noor asks.

The bluntness of her question throws me off. I hesitate, then say, "Of course, Noor. Why would you ask that?"

She hands the photos to me, and I look through them again. I wonder who they are and what their stories are. Leaning over and kissing my cheek, she says, "Don't worry. Marriage will protect you."

Allahu-Akbar. I'm being carried by two men from the mosque. I'm not myself, and I can't see clearly. Everything's out of whack; I feel out of control. I keep hearing a voice, haunting me, telling me something I can't understand. Then another voice comes, then another. *"Allahu-Akbar ... Allahu-Akbar ..."* I know that Allah is the greatest. Have I ever questioned that? Suddenly the voices become one and all I hear is "pink." I don't understand.

As the men take me home and place me on my bed, I glance at Shams, who is crying in distress. I remember when Shams' father told me that she did not want to marry me. She did not want to live as a conservative religious woman. I accepted her decision. But later, my family and I were invited for dinner at her family's home. The men and women sat in separate rooms. When I left the dining room to go to the washroom, Shams passed by me. I was brave enough to say to her, "I know you don't think highly of me. But I hope your opinion changes. I am not a horrible man. I have the respect of your family and hope you will give me a chance." Shams' face reddened as I spoke those words, then she walked away. Now I see in her face that she hasn't changed at all.

I look toward the doorway. The Angel Gabriel is there. He smiles and says, "We need to be alone now." I wonder if the men helping me have heard him, but they don't seem to notice.

"Thank you very much, brothers," I say. "I'm fine now. Please leave us."

Shams comes toward me, still crying. "Are you sure, darling?" She wipes the sweat off my brow.

I look at the impatient Gabriel, who whispers, "Now." What does this apparition, this Gabriel, want from me?

"Please, can you leave me? I need time alone," I say to my

lovely Shams. She looks at me with surprise.

When she leaves the room, I feel relieved. Gabriel then approaches, hovering over me to kiss my forehead.

"How are you feeling now?" he asks.

"I am well, *alhamdulillah*, thank you."

"I see you met her today."

"Who?"

"Abaddon."

"You know each other?"

"Of course."

"How?"

"Close your eyes."

I obey.

"Open your eyes," he says a moment later.

I'm no longer lying on my bed. I'm ethereal now, moving with freedom and ease. I melt as I move through the sun and then turn to ice as I float through the Arctic, becoming water as I swim in the ocean. And then I am dead, floating motionless upon the Dead Sea. Finally, my last breath having escaped me, my soul is transported to the heavens. I gaze down at mountains of stone and pools of water—raw nature. *Subhanallah.* Is this my new world? Or am I only a visitor?

Looking down again, I spot Gabriel and Abaddon standing in front of the Tree of Knowledge.

"What do we do now, Lord?" Gabriel asks.

Abaddon interjects, "Please don't listen to him. He just wants to spread love and peace. But he is ignoring Your original intentions."

Who are they talking to?

Gabriel turns to Abaddon, pausing before saying in a

quiet voice, "Don't you see there's been a lot of confusion, a lot of bloodshed, violence ..."

She snorts, then turns to the Tree and says, "Gabriel wants to take Your place, Lord. He ignores all Your books and wants to redefine knowledge."

"No! That's not what I'm trying to do."

She turns to face him. "You are lying, Gabriel."

"I am not lying! Can't you see what is happening to the world?"

Abaddon pauses for a moment, nods, and then looks back to the Tree. "Many people are transgressing, are manipulating the truth. Your truth."

Gabriel pushes Abaddon aside. "What is the truth?" he asks the Tree. "Why is it muddled with ambiguity?"

Abaddon says, "Do you hear what Gabriel is insinuating? He is denying Your truth!"

What is the truth? I wonder. I remain still and quiet, attempting to unravel the *hakika*, to uncover the mystery. And yet I feel restless.

"You love each and every human being. That is the truth, the one truth," Gabriel says before abruptly flying up next to me. He grabs my arm and pulls hard. Again I melt, then freeze, then turn to water. And then I fall to *nar jahanam*, to Hell.

I open my eyes and suddenly I am back on my bed. Gabriel is seated beside me, running his *werdy* fingers through my hair.

"Tell me I was dreaming. *Helm*."

He smiles, kisses my forehead again, and says, "No, you weren't dreaming. Did you see how Abaddon tries to manipulate God?"

"You were speaking to a tree."

"We were speaking to God."

"Where was He?"

"God is everywhere, all around us. Can you believe that witch? Promoting hatred and violence."

"What were you talking about?"

"Homosexuality."

"Oh, *astaghfirullah*."

Gabriel smiles, then says, "Why is it that people have such strong feelings on the topic?"

"Because it is forbidden, it is morally wrong. It is *haram*."

"What is wrong with two people falling in love?"

"There is nothing wrong with love."

"Then what is wrong with homosexuality?"

I look away, praying quietly. Please, Allah, forgive our sins.

"What are you doing?" he asks.

"I'm praying."

"Oh, come on, Ammar, why can't you wake up to reality?"

"I don't want to hear about it any longer. I don't want my son or anyone else influenced by this. I don't want to help the man who sent me the letter. I don't want to be associated with this. It's sick. It's disgusting."

Gabriel looks down, shaking his head slowly. "I'm sorry. I won't bother you anymore."

I am about to say something, but Gabriel disappears again.

I often wonder if I was meant to be in another body, to be someone else, or from a different family. Why did God choose me to be me? Looking out the window at the moon, I see Ali. I loved him more than anyone in the world, but does love mean anything? What's the point? The moon will disappear as always; the sun will come and go … Ah, why can't I sleep? I grab the clock and throw it to the floor.

In a few hours, I will get up, eat eggs and beans with Mohammed, and in the car, he will talk about marriage and women, as usual. I will nod as he natters on. Yes, Mohammed, I am going to marry; yes, Mohammed, I like women; yes, Mohammed, I am not *lotee*. Yes, Mohammed.

During class, I listen to the mathematics teacher drone on. Is he passionate about his profession? Does he even care? After half an hour of banal instruction he assigns us partners to work on equations. Mine is Waleed, who sits at the desk in front of me. Waleed never brushes his teeth, so his breath always smells like a mix of cigarettes and tea. It is unpleasant, but I force myself to ignore it. As we work together, I think of Ali, my old classroom partner, and his magical kisses.

I am relieved when the class is over. In the cafeteria, I get a sandwich and sit by myself on one of the benches. I hear footsteps approaching and turn to see a handsome young man with a guitar. He sits down beside me.

"Hello," he says. I cannot help staring at his face, which reminds me of Omar Khorshid, the late Egyptian movie star and guitarist. The young man is dressed in jeans and a tight T-shirt. Who is he? I've never seen him around campus.

"Hi," I croak, then blush. He must see how nervous

I am. I clear my throat and say, "I'm sorry. I think I almost choked on my sandwich."

He grins and starts tinkering with this guitar, then launches into a beautiful tune. I've heard it before, but I can't recall the name. He stops playing and raises his eyebrows at me.

"Please continue," I say.

As he plays, he asks, "What is your name?"

"Ramy."

He laughs and says, "It rhymes with my name."

"Which is ...?"

"Sammy." He glances at his watch. "I'm sorry, but I have to go."

"Where to?" I ask.

"I'm meeting some friends for a practice."

I want to ask him if I can go with him, but refrain. Instead, I say, "I hope to see you around."

He leaves and I'm alone again.

I've just been visited by an angel named Sammy.

Masha'Allah. Today is Friday, and every Friday, I feel special, like Allah has forgiven all my sins. After I wash my body with water, I am as clean and pure as a *malaak*. Sitting at the table, my son and I eat breakfast—eggs with beef sausages. Shams is in the kitchen, eating alone. Just after we were married, when I told her that she had to wear the *hejab*, she was displeased. But, as with our separation at meal times, she eventually agreed to it.

At the beginning of our relationship, we often argued about the smallest things because she could not accept the fact that there were rules that were bestowed upon us by God that we had to follow. Often, she would forget that she was married to a sheikh. One time she wanted to go out with her sister without a man to accompany them for protection. I did not allow that. She wouldn't speak to me for days. Thank God everything changed after the birth of Jaffar. We put our differences aside and focused on raising our son.

I sometimes feel like Job with his children. He loved his children more than any other living thing. But like Job, I fear that I will someday lose my son. That's life: sooner or later, we're all going to die. Odd that I only have these kinds of thoughts on the holy day of Friday. As I take a bite of sausage, I have a strange feeling that this could be my last one ... or Jaffar's. And I'm afraid.

Leaving my breakfast unfinished, I go to the living room and begin to read Qur'anic verses to bring some comfort to my soul. But sadness won't leave me alone; it overwhelms me. I finally make a decision.

When Jaffar and I arrive at the mosque, I try to forget the awkwardness of what happened last time; try to pretend it never took place. I sit and quietly read the Qur'an for the ten minutes before my lecture.

The gentle strumming of the guitar comforts me as I soar among the clouds, a bird with a thousand wings. I look down and see Sammy.

A knock on the door disturbs my dream.

"Ramy, wake up! We have to go to Friday prayers," Mohammed says.

Why can't I sleep in for a change? Why can't I dream about Sammy?

"Ramy, are you awake?"

I get up. "Yes, yes."

"Good. Well, let's go. We're already late."

I grab a towel and clean underwear and head to the bathroom for my morning shower.

Ya rab. I look around and see the mighty words of Allah painted on the walls. It's as if I fully understand these words for the first time. And something is different about the mosque. Has someone moved a painting? Is something missing? Among the faithful, Jaffar sits cross-legged, quietly talking to a man beside him. Like a pharaoh, I perch upon my throne-like pedestal, looking down at my people as they await judgment. I open a small notebook, put on my glasses, and recite: "Dear brothers and sisters, I've had a request to discuss ..." I clear my throat. "... to discuss homosexuality."

The hot water gushes from the showerhead, trickling down my body, washing it and my soul clean. I think of Sammy; I hear the beautiful notes from his guitar and visualize his magical hands upon me. But I cannot fall in love again. I must not.

I clear my throat yet again. "Homosexuality is unlawful in Islam, my brothers and sisters. It is neither accepted by the state nor by Islamic society. The Qur'an clearly states that it is unjust, it is unnatural, a transgression and a crime. It's *haram. Haram!* I have some verses here." Jaffar looks confused, but when our eyes meet, he nods with understanding.

The truth is, he made my heart skip a beat like Ali did when I met him the first time. Is it because I am weak and cannot control my heart? I don't want to fall in love just to lose yet another. I don't want Sammy to face the same fate as Omar Khorshid, the Egyptian celebrity who was killed in a car accident, perhaps by design. But I can imagine being with Sammy ...

The men in front of me have looks of discomfort on their faces, even disgust. This is a topic to avoid at all times. But I've begun and I must go on. *Astaghfirullah.*

"We must make sure our children are aware of the teachings of Islam. And ... and it is very important to discuss. Our children must be clear about this problem." I pause to sip some water.

I feel Sammy putting his hand on my chest, feeling my heartbeat. He kisses my lips, then our tongues begin to explore each other's.

"'If two men among you commit indecency, punish them both. If they repent and mend their ways, let them be. God is forgiving and merciful,' the Qur'an tells us in verse four-sixteen."

He is pulling my hair, kissing me roughly. I am his slave; he is my master. I am his guitar; he plays me—

"Ramy, we're late!" shouts Mohammed through the door.

"Yes, yes, give me a minute!"

I take a deep breath and look around, then set my eyes upon Jaffar. "Yes, my dear brothers and sisters, the Qur'an clearly condemns homosexuality. Here is another quote. God says: 'You lust after men instead of women. Truly, you are a degenerate people.'"

In the car, Mohammed is sweating. For him, missing Friday prayers is like desecrating one of the five pillars. He is sure he is not a good Muslim.

"What were you doing in there?" he demands.

"I was taking a shower."

"Even girls don't take as long."

What's that supposed to mean?

Outside the mosque, Mohammed parks the car and hurries away. I follow after him. The sheikh is already halfway through his lecture. When Mohammed and I join the other men on the floor, we listen to the sheikh as he continues to speak:

"My dear brothers and sisters, I don't think I need to stress enough how much we need to teach our children about this. Don't be afraid to tell your son or daughter how disgusting homosexuality is."

I see the young man who has just come in and wonder: Is he a good Muslim? Then, in the distance, Abaddon appears with a grin on her face.

"*As-salamu alaykum,*" I say, ending my lecture.

I don't think God is willing to help me. I mean, if His supposed messengers are not willing to help, then no one should blame me for "transgressing." I am who I am, and if nobody is willing to help me, why should I be different? I turn to Mohammed and tell him I want to go home.

"But we just got here."

"Please, Mohammed."

"Wait. I have a few questions for the sheikh." He gets up and abandons me, leaving me alone among strangers. I don't have a single friend here at the mosque. But I am concerned. Why does

Mohammed want to talk with the sheikh?

Alhamdulillah. I am relieved that this lecture is done. I just want to go home and take a nice hot bath. As I go to collect Jaffar, a man approaches me and says hello. I return his greeting.

"I'm sorry I arrived late. But I take it that today's topic was about homosexuality."

"Yes, brother. It was."

"Should we be concerned as a community?"

I pause, unsure how to respond. "I wouldn't say so, but it's good to be informed," I finally reply. I look over at Jaffar, who is sitting quietly and reading the Qur'an. Suddenly Gabriel appears overhead, flies up to Jaffar, and leans over to kiss him.

"No!" I shout and run toward Jaffar, but by the time I get to him, Gabriel has vanished. I am gasping when I ask, "Are you okay, *habibi*?"

"I'm fine, Baba. What's wrong?"

I sigh and smile at him.

The drive home is silent. I stare out the window as Mohammed recites Qur'anic verses, glancing over at me every few moments. I can tell he wants to say something, but I don't wish to push him.

He finally begins to talk, then stops himself. Instead, he puts on an Oum Kalthoum CD. Mohammed is a fan of the classical Egyptian singer and listens to her every day. We have very different tastes in music. I'm more into Omar Khorshid and Amr Diab, even though Mohammed thinks these modern pop singers are "soulless."

"You know I don't like Oum Kalthoum," I say.

He looks at me. "You know I don't like homosexuals."

My mouth goes dry. I try to stay calm.

"What do you mean?" I ask.

"You know what I mean."

"Mohammed, if you have something to say, say it."

Mohammed swerves the car violently; the tires squeal. He slams on the brakes suddenly, and I lurch forward. After catching my breath, I say, "What's going on?"

"I need to know the truth. Are you…? God, I can't even say the word." Staring straight ahead, he slams his hands against the steering wheel. "Are you?"

"Am I what?" I feel the panic beginning to set in.

"Don't act stupid, Ramy. Tell me the truth!" He turns and grabs my shirt collar. "Are you *lotee*?"

"No!" I say defiantly.

"Don't lie to me!"

"I'm not *lotee*! I'm not *lotee*! *Wallah*, I'm not …" I can feel tears beginning to form in my eyes.

Mohammed lets go of me, then sighs. "In the name of God … I just wanted to make sure."

He puts the car in gear and continues to drive. I'm sure he's heard only what he wants to hear. As we drive along in silence, I think of what might have transpired instead:

I'm in the car with Mohammed, but something isn't right. He looks at me, stops the car, and says, "Tell me the truth! Are you …?" He can't even say the words. He knows that I know what he wants me to say. And he is afraid.

"Are you *lotee*?" he finally asks. And I nod. I simply nod. He says, "I knew all along. How can I look at you and not feel sick?" He spits in my face. Or it might have gone like this:

Mohammed is driving, and I feel uncomfortable as I sit

beside him. He says, "I want to know the truth." But I don't know how to answer him.

"What truth?" I finally ask.

"Are you *lotee*?" he asks.

"Yes."

"You're *lotee*."

"Yes."

"I've always known." A moment of silence follows. He smiles, leans over, and kisses my cheek.

"I've always known."

Subhanallah walhamdulilah wala ilaha illallah wallahu akbar. Thank God for everything. I have just finished my nighttime prayers and am ready to go to sleep. But first I go to Jaffar's room to kiss him goodnight. His blanket lies on the floor, and he is tossing and turning. This is unsettling—what is Jaffar going through? He has never opened up to me. Maybe I need to try harder. I don't ask about his personal life, I just assume that he is still an innocent. But he is growing up.

I pick up the blanket and cover his shivering body. Then I sit down beside him and recite some Qur'anic verses, praying to God to protect him. Looking at him, I remember my younger self.

When I was ten years old, my father also used to read me Qur'anic verses as I lay on my bed. The words of God brought comfort to my soul. My father would kiss my forehead, and then I'd fall asleep. He made me feel happy. He made me feel good.

Allah yehafthak ya ebny ul aziz. May God keep you safe. I kiss Jaffar and leave his room in silence. When I enter our bedroom, I am surprised to see that Shams is still awake. She smiles at me and I smile back.

"What's keeping you awake, darling?" I ask quietly.

"I'm waiting for you."

"Ah ..."

She looks at me, her face bright. She isn't wearing the *hejab*; her long, beautiful red hair falls past her shoulders.

"How was your day?" she asks.

"Long. But how are you? What did you do today?"

"I'm good. I spent the day with my sister. We went grocery shopping."

"How is she?"

"She's fine, but Salah isn't feeling well. She took him to the hospital. He had stomach flu."

"I pray he gets better."

She sighs as she reaches over to stroke my hair. Then she kisses me.

"Are you all right?" she asks when I don't respond.

"Yes. Just tired."

"Do you need a massage?"

"Oh, that'd be lovely."

"Lie on your stomach. I will make you feel better."

I take my shirt off and do as she says. Shams places her hands on my back and begins to knead my muscles. Every ache, every pain begins to dissipate.

"I love you, *habibi*." She sighs and kisses my back, then I am shocked when she begins to lick it. I feel tremors tickling my spine. I turn over.

"Ammar," Shams whispers, then kisses my lips. "I haven't felt this way in a long time." She unbuttons her nightgown and slides out of it; she is so beautiful. She moves my hand to touch her body, wanting me to ...

But no. I am not here. Instead, I am in a room where two men are locked in a naked embrace. Gabriel hovers in a corner near the ceiling. Suddenly stones of fire drop upon the lovers, and I watch in horror as the fire consumes them, reducing them to ashes. Gabriel, standing behind me now, asks, "What do you know of the people of Lot?"

"I have memorized the verses."

"I know you have."

I approach the bed and run my hands through the ashes, now cold.

"What does God say in the Qur'an? 'And remember Lot, when he said to his people: Do you commit the worst sin such as none preceding you has committed in the *Aalameen*, mankind, and jinns? Verily, you practise your lusts on men instead of women. Nay, but you are a people transgressing beyond bounds by committing great sins.'"

The little creature grins at me. "I'm impressed that you remember the words so accurately," he says.

"My father reminded me of these verses regularly," I say. "May his soul rest in peace. He hated *lotees*."

"Do you?"

I pause for a moment and stare down at the ashes of those who have sinned. I realize that this is God's will; it is His decision to punish those who disobeyed His wishes. He has given us life, and all He asks in return is for us to do His bidding.

"I'm sure you believe as your father did before you," Gabriel says.

"You make it sound like that's bad."

Gabriel's wings flutter. "Ammar, I'm not saying it's bad to follow in your father's footsteps, but do you hate homosexuals?"

"Yes!" I spit out. "Isn't it obvious? And no, I will not help the letter writer!"

Gabriel asks whether I know the reasons for Allah's punishment against the people of Lot.

"I know the truth. It's in the Qur'an."

"The truth is in the Qur'an, but it is ambiguous."

"No!" I say. "It's very clear."

Gabriel grabs my hand, taking me with him as he flies away.

"Let me go!" I demand.

"I will show you the truth."

"No, I don't want to go!"

"I'm sorry, Ammar. You don't really have a choice."

Then he lets go of me and I fall from the sky, landing on the roof of a house. I am ice-cold, but the roof melts, and I fall into the house. Slumping to the floor, I am burning in *nar jahanam*.

A boy with long golden hair, dressed in a plain white robe, sits on a bed. As he is about to cover himself with a blanket, a door opens and slams shut, startling me. I watch. Two men stand on either side of the boy's bed. Speaking in Hebrew, the boy yells at them. Their faces are covered with beards and moustaches as red as blood. One of them laughs; the other says something, again in Hebrew. I don't understand a word of it. But I don't need to understand; their body language fills me with dread. One grabs the boy and cuffs his wrists together. The other rips the boy's robe off as he cries out. They push the boy's face against the wall. I shut my eyes and pray in silence.

"God punished the people of Lot because of this incident. Don't ever forget it." I hear Gabriel's voice inside my head. I block out the sounds around me.

I open my eyes; the boy is lying on the floor, blood spilling from his backside. I go to him. The men are gone. *Astaghfirullah.*

"Are you all right?" I ask, knowing that he won't understand me. He puts his hand on mine, pleading with me in Hebrew.

"I'll help you. Don't worry." I go to the door and twist the knob, but it is locked. "Help! Help!" I yell.

After banging on the door and calling for help for several moments, I turn back to the boy. I am confused and overwhelmed.

What do I do? The boy grabs my arm, then says something incomprehensible to me before he slumps back and stops breathing. Suddenly the door opens again and the two men return. They talk loudly, their voices threatening. One grabs me by the shoulder while the other pulls my face toward his and then kisses me. *Astaghfirullah!* I shut my eyes and pray to God to save me. I am shivering as they pull off my clothes and push me against the wall. I can no longer feel my body. I hear whispers. The colour *werdy* is all around and begins to consume me.

Drowning in a sea of pink, I struggle, fighting to make it to shore. Only when I am there am I able to breathe again. I look up to see the pink on Shams' lips as she leans over to kiss me. I gasp, push her away, and head toward the bathroom. I undress and jump into the tub, turning the hot water on to cleanse the filth from my body. By the time I finish and get dressed, I feel holy again. But when I return to our room, Shams is in bed, her back toward me. I lie on my side of the bed and turn off the light.

I count one, two, three, four, five ... It's useless. I can't sleep. There is a knock at the door. It is Mohammed. I wonder why he is here at this hour.

"Yes, Mohammed."

"Did I wake you?"

"No, it's okay." He turns on the light. I see an envelope in his hand.

"What's this?" I ask, pointing at the envelope as I sit up.

"I want to show these to you again." He opens the envelope and hands me the same three photographs of the women he had shown me before. I look at the first one.

"Her name is Yassmine."

"I remember."

"She lives a few blocks from here. Her father owns a grocery store. Noor says she's a wonderful woman."

I look at her again and feel sorry for her. If I were to marry her, it would end in disaster.

The second photograph is of a woman with a ponytail and wide smile.

"This is Lamia. She's graduating from medical school soon. Noor says she is very intelligent and outspoken." I shrug my shoulders.

Mohammed shows me the last photograph. "This is Jameela," he says, which means beautiful in Arabic. And she is very beautiful, indeed.

"What do you think?"

"She is like her name." I think I succeed in convincing Mohammed that I am attracted to her.

"Good. I will let you think about them. Choose one, and Noor will set up a time for a meeting."

"Okay."

Mohammed looks at me, then leans over and kisses my cheek. "I love you, Ramy. So much. And I can't wait to hold your first-born in my arms."

I smile back at him, not wanting to ruin his moment of happiness. After all, he has taken good care of me all these years. I can't hurt his feelings.

"All right, *habibi*. Goodnight." After he leaves the room, I wonder if *habibi* really means anything. Does he really love me? Or does his love depend on whether I get married and live a normal life?

I lie down on my bed and close my eyes.

I am standing outside a house, holding a bouquet of roses. I knock, and Yassmine answers. Her thick ebony hair shines in the sunlight.

"Hello, Ramy," she says and shakes my hand, then takes the bouquet as I escort her toward the car.

"So, you're the daughter of Razaq?" I ask.

"Yes. You've been to the store before?"

I nod. "I go there a lot with my sister-in-law and brother."

She nods. "My father is a hard-working man. After all these years, he still refuses to hire a helper. Just he and my brothers take care of the shop."

In my mind, we are then seated in a restaurant. As we look at the menu, she asks me, "So tell me, are you the marriage type?"

"What do you mean?"

"Are you looking to get married? Isn't that why we're here right now?"

I am speechless, but fortunately, a group of musicians

begins to play. A belly dancer emerges from behind a screen, her jewellery glittering in the dim lighting.

"Look at her," says Yassmine. "She's an artist. The men admire her, maybe they even want to sleep with her. But at the same time, they make fun of her and degrade her." She sighs. "Our society is so judgmental."

"I agree with you."

"I mean, people like to talk. They like to gossip. They like to make fun of and degrade others. Why do they do that, Ramy? I don't get it."

"People are cruel," I say.

"I have a friend," she continues. "One of my really close friends. She's a belly dancer too. And people look down on her, even though they enjoy watching her. Such hypocrites."

"What about her family?"

"When they found out, her brother and her cousins beat her up in front of all the neighbours. My friend was humiliated. She was broken. We lost touch, and I don't know what happened to her. I heard from some people that she got married right after. Not by choice, probably."

"Well ... I'm sorry to hear that."

"Ramy, I'm not sure I ever want to marry ..."

I can see that Yassmine feels guilty for confessing this, but it makes me happy.

"Don't worry," I say. "It doesn't bother me."

She smiles. "Well, of course it doesn't. We both know ... you're not interested in marriage."

I sigh. "Well, I suppose I can't help it."

"It's not your fault. But we live in a country that forces us to conform to traditional ways."

I admire her. In a strange way, I even feel attracted to her.

I am awakened from my reverie when Mohammed once again knocks on my door, telling me he's ready to go to school. He comes in, dressed for work. "I hope you had some time to think about the pictures."

"Not yet, *habibi*. Give me a few more days."

"All right. But don't take too long. They will not wait forever."

"Then what should I do?"

"Just pick one. It doesn't really matter who."

Choosing a wife based on a photograph alone is ridiculous, but I keep my opinion to myself. I realize that this is our tradition. You see a photograph, and if she is pretty, she will make a good wife—a facile assumption. But many successful marriages begin this way. If I were a heterosexual man, I would want to get to know the woman first: her personality, goals, views on life.

"Why are you quiet?"

"I'm just thinking about women."

"Good man."

Oh, yes—thinking about them, dreaming about them, fantasizing about them. It fascinates me that Mohammed seems to buy all that talk.

Later, in class, I think again about Mohammed's obsession over marrying me off. When will it end? And then I hear a faint melody through the open window.

After class, I track down the source of the music. Through an open door, I see two men, one playing guitar and the other a violin. The guitar player is Sammy. Oh god, he is beautiful.

The music comes to an end when Sammy looks up and sees me. At first I feel like ducking my head, then realize how stupid that would look.

"Hi," I say awkwardly.

"What are you doing here?" he asks, smiling.

"I was ... You sound great."

"Come on in," he says, opening the door wide.

Inside, Sammy introduces me to the violinist, Firas.

"You're brilliant," I tell Firas, but I'm thinking of Sammy.

"Any requests?" Sammy asks.

I know they're going to laugh, but I really want to hear one particular song: "My Heart Will Go On." When I tell them what it is, I'm surprised that they take me seriously. Sammy begins to play the intro, and Firas joins in. I shut my eyes and imagine myself on the ship. I imagine that I'm Rose and Sammy is Jack, holding me as I let go and fly. When the movie played on Iraqi television, I was transfixed. It convinced me that I would rather die in the arms of a lover than die alone in a world that imprisons me in silence.

When the song ends, my eyes are fixed on Sammy. Firas must have noticed because he quickly packs his violin up and finds an excuse to leave. My heart begins to pound so loudly, I'm afraid Sammy will hear it.

"So, you liked our music?" Sammy asks. I know I'm blushing.

"I could listen to you play guitar all day."

"I don't know about that," he says, smiling.

Suddenly I feel brave. "I was thinking maybe we could have dinner together sometime?"

"Hmm. I have a concert tomorrow, actually. If you want to come, I'd be happy to see you then."

"Oh really? I ..." I am at a loss for words. He wants to see me?

"I'll take that as a yes," he says, laughing.

Before I can respond, the door opens and a young woman walks in. She smiles at Sammy as she reaches for his hand. Who is she?

"All right, buddy, I have to go now," Sammy says. He pulls a flyer out of his guitar case. "Here's the address for tomorrow's concert."

Then they leave together. I am alone again.

At home, I lock myself in my room, lie on the bed, and vow to give up on love once and for all. It hurts too much. I don't know if I should bother to go to the concert. I should have learned from my past experience with Ali. But when I wrestle with my heart, I can't help myself. I cannot triumph. I close my eyes, and within minutes, I fall asleep.

"What's the matter?" a female voice whispers.

I look up and see that I'm in a doctor's office. I sit on a chair and facing me is a woman with a ponytail, wearing a white lab coat.

"I'm Dr Lamia. And you must be Ramy."

"Yes." I reach for her hand. "Nice to meet you, Dr Lamia."

"I hope I look better in person. I don't photograph well."

"Uh ... right. So, what kind of doctor are you?"

"I'm a family doctor."

She places her stethoscope on my chest. "Are you feeling well? You seem sad."

"I'm just thinking about a lot of things. But I'm okay, thanks."

"Good." She puts the stethoscope on the table and sits down across from me. "So, what's bothering you?"

"I'm just ... sad."

"You're in love?"

"No, of course not!"

"It's okay. You don't have to get into details. We've all been in love before. It's normal. You don't have to hide it."

"I wouldn't say I'm in love with her. I just have a crush on her."

The doctor's eyes widen in surprise. "Her?"

"Yes," I lie. "Yes."

"Look, there's one thing you should know: I'm the last person to judge you."

I let out a sigh. "It's difficult, you know, I—"

"I know what you mean. My brother felt the same."

"Your brother?"

"Ahmed. He was gay also, and he came out to me when he was young. I told him that he couldn't live like this. He had to marry."

"See, that's the problem. You should've accepted him"

"I did accept him!" she interrupts. "But I was being realistic. My parents were so conservative, they didn't let us do anything. I wanted to be an actress, wanted to star in movies. But no, they started threatening me and kept pushing me to go to medical school."

"I'm sorry. I know how you feel."

"In other places, you might be able to be free and be whoever you want to be. But not in Iraq. You can't be gay. It's always about family honour and respect."

"So what happened to your brother? Did your parents find out?"

"Unfortunately, they did. Rumours went around that my brother was caught sleeping with the neighbours' boy. I was worried they'd kill Ahmed, but he fled the country, to Turkey. I haven't heard much from him since." She pauses. "I miss him very much, my little brother. I hope he's okay and in a better place."

I get up and give her a hug. "I'm so sorry."

"What are you going to do?" she asks.

"Honestly? I don't know."

"Trust me, take my advice. Just get married to a woman unless you're planning to leave the country."

"I had the opportunity to escape, but I couldn't. I couldn't hurt my family."

"I can help you."

"What do you mean?"

Instead of answering, she startles me by kissing my neck, then down to my chest. The hairs on my arms rise; I've got goosebumps, and I feel a stirring in my groin. But a knot of nervousness also begins to tighten in my chest. I wake up in a cold, cold sweat.

I work up the nerve to go to Sammy's concert. Waiting for him to perform, my heart beats like a *dabke* drum; Sammy is beating on it. Glancing around, I see the girl he was with before, sitting beside an older woman; they are both wearing *hejab*s. Who is she? His girlfriend or fiancée or wife? I wish she would disappear. Is that too much to ask?

Finally, the lights dim. Sitting in the darkness, I close my eyes as he starts to play, and I'm mesmerized. Then, before I know it, though, the lights are back on, and he is taking his bows.

When Sammy leaves the stage, the girl and the older woman leave too, presumably to join him backstage. Jealousy overcomes me. Soon everyone else is gone; I am alone and realize that I am wallowing in self-pity. I should act, do something, anything.

Then a tap on my shoulder startles me. I turn to see Sammy.

"Hi," he says with a grin. "Thanks for coming tonight."

"You play so well!"

He shakes his head. I feel awkward, trying to think of something else to say. "So ... who was that woman with you?" I finally ask.

"What woman?"

"The one who left with you the other day, at school. I saw her here tonight."

He laughs. "That's my sister."

My heart lightens. "I thought she was your fiancée!"

"That's funny. Don't worry!"

Why would he think that I'd be worried?

"What are you doing now?" I ask.

"They're waiting for me. I think I'll call it a night."

"No!" I blurt out, mentally kicking myself.

"Is something wrong?"

"No, I meant ... I don't really have anything to do right now. Do you want to ... go for dinner or something?"

"Dinner sounds lovely."

"Really?"

"But I have to drive my mother and sister home first. Do you have a car?"

"No."

"Then come with me."

Mohammed had offered me a ride to the concert, but I took a taxi instead. I didn't want to answer any more of his questions. And I didn't want to raise any suspicions in him since I was doing my best to rebuild the trust between us. After all, Mohammed is happy with me now because he believes that I'll be getting married soon and will have a family of my own.

In Sammy's car, I ride up front while Sammy's mother and sister are in the backseat. I can feel his mother glaring from behind me. A friend of mine once told me that mothers could smell homosexuals from a hundred miles away. I wonder if she has such a talent.

"How do you two know each other?" she eventually asks.

"Sammy and I both go to Baghdad University," I answer.

"Ah," she says and falls silent again. His sister stifles a giggle.

When we arrive at their house, the two women get out of the car; Sammy waits until they safely enter their apartment building before turning to me.

"Where do you want to go?" he asks.

"Anywhere." I mean it. We could be stranded in a desert, and I'd be okay with it.

"I'll take you somewhere special," Sammy says.

We drive along the Qadisaya Expressway, past the sword monument and the victory arch, to the local market area, where all the cheap shops are. There, food carts in the street serve regional Iraqi foods, such as *pache*, lamb's head and feet, or falafel and beans.

"What do you feel like eating?" he asks me. "It will be my treat."

"Thank you! I love *lessan*," I tell him, pointing at the cart that sells sheep and cow tongue sandwiches. Sammy parks the car and we walk toward the street vendor.

"So, which do you prefer, the cow or the sheep?"

I laugh. "The sheep."

"Good choice."

Sammy orders two lamb tongue sandwiches from an older

man and his two young sons. He hands me one and says, "Enjoy."

"Thanks, *habibi*."

We walk down the street as we eat our delicious sandwiches. Sammy greets a middle-aged man in front of a grocery store, then explains, "Sajjad is my boss. I work for him a few days a week here to help out my family."

"Do you have any other siblings?" I ask

"Just Rawan, my sister. My mom works day and night, making clothes. How else can we survive in this day and age?"

"What about your father?"

"He passed away when I was young. He died during the first war."

"I'm sorry to hear that. May Allah bless his soul."

"Amen."

As I take the last bite of my sandwich, Sammy asks, "What about you? Who do you live with?"

"My brother and his wife. My father was killed by Saddam. And my mom—"

"Fuck Saddam."

We walk a few more steps in silence, both of us momentarily lost in thought about our families and what Iraq used to be.

"I just want to finish school and get out of here," Sammy finally says.

"What about marriage?" I can't help myself from asking.

"Marriage is the last thing on my mind right now. When I'm financially ready, I'll find myself a good wife."

Of course he will. It's the Iraqi way.

Sammy drops me off back at home. In my room, I shut my eyes. Soon I hear *maqam* music and see myself seated inside a nightclub. At the tables beside me are wealthy men, smoking cigars and drinking alcohol. They roar with excitement when a beautiful woman appears on stage, her long hair covered with a glittery scarf. From her eyes alone, I realize that the dancer is Yassmine. Dancing to the music of the *ney*, the Arabian flute, and the *dabke*, the drums, her hips move and shake, but her eyes are somehow fixed on mine.

After her performance, Yassmine comes over to the table and sits down next to me.

"Now you know my secret," she says, smiling.

"You know my secret, too."

She leans over and kisses me on the cheek.

I wake up from the dream when I hear some noise in the kitchen. There I find Noor sitting at the table, crying.

"Noor, are you okay?" I ask.

She looks surprised to see me. "Oh, I didn't know you were awake."

"Why are you crying? What's wrong?"

"I can't sleep. Don't worry. You go back to bed."

"Noor, please ... Did you and Mohammed fight?"

"No! Not at all! I was just ... dreaming about you having kids one day. I can't wait for that day."

I know that Noor isn't telling me the truth. My heart tells me she had been dreaming yet again about having her own children. "Why can't you just adopt?" I ask.

"You know it's not that easy, Ramy."

"Why not? You can give a poor child love and a home. Why is it *haram*?"

"It's not *haram*. We could've adopted a child, but ... people talk."

"Who cares what other people think?"

"They would look down upon us."

"People talk all the time, Noor, you shouldn't care what they say."

"I must go to bed now." She kisses my forehead and says goodnight.

In the morning, Mohammed and Noor are seated at the table. She shows no sign of her distress from the previous night, but both she and Mohammed look as if they are waiting for me.

"Ramy," Mohammed says. "Come and sit down."

My heart begins to race. Now what? As I sit, Mohammed says, "Do you remember Jameela?"

"I remember seeing her photo, yes. What about her?"

"Noor spoke with Jameela's mother, and she's invited us all over for dinner."

"When?"

"This evening. Come with me, Ramy," he says as he gets up from the table.

I feel a sense of dread come over me, but I don't have a say in the matter. Mohammed leads me to his room. He can't seem to contain his excitement as he rifles through his closet.

"What are you doing, Hamoody?" I know he likes me to call him that, my pet name for him.

He pulls out a suit. "I hope this will fit you. I want you to wear it tonight."

I try it on; it fits me, although the pants feel a little too tight. I imagine leaning over to shake hands with Jameela and— rip! Maybe Jameela would disapprove of me if my pants ripped, and then maybe Mohammed and Noor would stop bugging me about finding a wife. Mohammed sits on his bed watching as I look at myself in the mirror.

"Look, I need you to act mature and responsible at dinner. I want you ..."

I know what he is trying to say. He wants me to be manly, to act honourably. "I just want you to be good," he continues. "Try to impress the woman and her family."

"I ... will," I say reluctantly.

That night, as I am getting dressed, that trapped feeling creeps up on me again. My brother and his wife have sacrificed so much for me. I owe it to them to make sacrifices too. Looking in the mirror, I try to really see myself. Am I truly homosexual? How can I be straight if it's only Sammy I want now, and before that, Ali?

In the car, I sit in the back seat, quietly observing Mohammed and Noor as they chat. I realize that, after all these years, they are still in love. I wonder how this could be possible when they don't have any children. Aren't children what keep a husband and wife together? I find it odd that Mohammed and Noor rarely fight. Is that normal in marriage? I remember that if my aunt Houda and uncle Tareq weren't fighting, there was something wrong. One day, when we went to visit them, they were shouting at each other, and from the other room, we heard dishes breaking. Would Sammy and I fight like that?

When we arrive at Jameela's house, Noor gets out first. Mohammed turns to me and says, "Look, Ramy, you know what to do. Be yourself, but act respectfully."

How can I be myself and show respect when I don't feel it? But I will try.

An old man answers the door. He must be Jameela's father, Ghassan. Mohammed and the old man shake hands and kiss each other four times on the cheeks. Traditions are traditions in the Middle East. Mohammed turns and introduces us. It is my turn to shake his hand and kiss his cheeks.

"It is a pleasure to meet you, *Amo*," I say. Then Jameela's mother comes and shares four kisses with Noor before leading us inside to the living room, which is beautifully decorated, with leather couches and abstract paintings on the walls. I am particularly drawn to one, composed of dark forms in shades of grey and black.

"Jameela painted it," her mother, Najwa, says, noticing my interest.

"It's beautiful," I reply.

I sit beside Noor while Mohammed and Ghassan chat about politics and the chaotic situation here. When Jameela's mother goes to the kitchen, Noor, like a mother herself, turns to me and lightly touches my cheek.

"This is good, Ramy," she says, obviously hopeful that the evening will end well.

Finally, Jameela herself enters the room with Najwa, carrying a tray with cups of juice. But Jameela doesn't look like what I had imagined. She is wearing a long-sleeved blouse and a long skirt, and her head is covered with a pink *hejab*. Najwa explains that Jameela has recently decided to wear it.

"Congratulations," Noor says with a smile. In Muslim society, it is something to be proud of. Before the war, few women wore them, but since then, it has become much more common, especially with young women pressured to do so by their parents. I wonder if Jameela's *hejab* is a genuine representation of her beliefs or something else. If I am to marry her, I need to get to know her better. She sits down on the couch next to me.

"My mother says you like my paintings."

"They're wonderful. How long have you been painting?"

"Since I was six."

"I'm amazed at how ... dark they are."

"How do they make you feel?" she asks.

"They make me feel ... lonely, actually."

"Me too. I mean, that's how I felt when I painted them."

"It's interesting what loneliness can do to a person," I say. She smiles at me. I think she is interested, but all I feel is panic.

Dinner seems to go well; I am polite and courteous and say all the right things to Jameela, *Amo* Ghassan, and *Khala* Najwa. Mohammed and Noor seem happy. On the drive home, they talk about what a wonderful girl Jameela is, but I just nod. Yes, Jameela is beautiful. Yes, she's nice, yes, she's talented. Yes, she has wonderful parents. Yes, yes, yes.

When Mohammed and Noor go to bed, I lie on my bed listening to the ticking of the clock. Unable to sleep, I go to the bathroom and take off my clothes. I stare at myself naked in the mirror. There is hair all over my body. I turn around and look over my shoulder; there is even more on my back. I have to get rid of it.

I run the electric razor roughly over my body. It cuts into my skin—the pain brings tears to my eyes, and spots of red begin to appear on my back. The hairs fall to the floor at my feet. The razor is so loud—what if Mohammed or Noor knock on the door? What would I tell them? I'm pretty sure Mohammed would see it as a sissy thing to do and beat the shit out of me. He'd tell me how body hair is a sign of manliness.

But I continue to buzz away until there is not a single hair left. My skin is red and there are nicks and cuts, but it is worth it. If I ever end up in bed with Sammy ... I imagine him kissing my back, smooth and hairless.

Ya rab ehdena ya rab. God, please guide us to the right path. I lie on the bed as Shams sits at her makeup table, facing the mirror. I watch as she slowly applies pink lipstick. Shams then stands up and unzips her dress, slowly revealing her body. I am hypnotized … by the colour pink.

I wake up in the middle of the night from a bad dream and go to the kitchen for some water. Gabriel is waiting for me there.

"What are you doing here?" I ask.

"I came to see how you're doing."

"I was doing fine until you came."

"Ammar, you have to admit, I'm not such a bad angel after all."

"What do you want from me, Gabriel?"

"I know what woke you up."

"Good, you know. Now, leave me alone."

"It's your father, isn't it?"

"Can we not talk about him, please?"

"But did you really want to become a sheikh?"

"Yes, of course."

"I don't think so. You only became a sheikh because your father was one."

"Maybe. But I'm happy with my life, and I'm sure my son will be too."

"So you're a tyrant just like your father?"

"My father was never a tyrant. He wanted the best for me."

Suddenly, Gabriel transforms into my very own father, smiling through his bushy white beard. He approaches me and gathers me in his arms. "You have to face the truth," he says. "You have to pray to God always."

"What are you doing here, father?"

"The truth, *ebny*, is the most beautiful thing in life."

"What truth are you talking about?"

He kisses my forehead. "You're a good son, *ebny*. I wronged you. I hurt you. I just want to say … I'm sorry."

Before I can respond, my father returns to the form of Gabriel. I resist the urge to cry.

"Will you forgive him?" Gabriel asks. I don't reply. I stand up and am about to leave the kitchen when Gabriel begs me to stay.

"What do you want from me?" I demand.

"You didn't answer my question."

I turn around to face him. "Look, Gabriel, please leave me in peace. I don't want you to come here again."

"Do you forgive your father?" he asks, ignoring my plea.

"He didn't do anything to me for which I have to forgive him."

"Are you sure about that?"

I shake my head. This time I can't stop the tears from flowing. "Please leave me alone," I beg.

Gabriel comes nearer. "God will never forgive him for what he did. He was supposed to be a good father, yet he beat you constantly," he says.

"But he was a good father. Sometimes, I deserved to be beaten."

"He was cruel to you."

"He's my father."

Suddenly, Jaffar enters the room.

"Jaffar, what are you doing up?" I see that he's been crying.

"Baba, I can't sleep."

"What's wrong, *ebny*?" He comes toward me and puts his head on my shoulder, sobbing.

"What is it? What happened?" I hate seeing him like this.

"I had a bad dream, Baba."

I hold him in a tight embrace. My beautiful son. If only he knew how much I loved him. "We all have nightmares. But it's only a dream." I wipe the tears from his cheeks and hug him again. "What did you dream about?" I ask.

He pauses, then says, "You were in it, Baba. You were beating me."

"Beating you? Jaffar, I would never do that."

"You said, 'If you don't do what I say, I will kill you.'"

"Jaffar, I would never say something like that to you. Never!"

"You ... you ..." He begins to sob again.

I hold Jaffar in my arms and reassure him that everything will be all right, that I will always protect him from harm. I turn to see the sun's morning rays coming through the window and pray for God to protect us.

Through the windshield, I stare at the beautiful Babylonian sun as we drive to school. I look at my brother; his attention is focused on the road. Studying his face, I try to understand what is going on in his mind. He is usually talkative, but this morning he seems troubled.

"Noor found something that belongs to you," he finally says.

"What?"

"Your razor. Why do you need that?"

"Lots of men have them."

"And you left hair all over the sink and floor. Noor wasn't happy about that."

"I'm sorry."

"You'd better apologize to her."

"I'll make sure to clean it up better next time."

"You know men don't do that. They don't shave or wax. Only women."

I sigh. What's the point? Mohammed has his own ideas and refuses to change them, no matter what. So I just don't bother; I keep silent.

After class, I want to find Sammy. I discover him practising in the band room, plucking away on his guitar. But when I enter, he doesn't even look up.

"Hi, Sammy," I say.

He doesn't reply.

"Sammy?" I try again.

Finally, he turns to me. "Sorry. I didn't realize you were here."

"Are you okay?"

He takes a deep breath and sighs. "I had an argument with

my family. They're pressuring me to get married."

"But you said you don't want to."

"I know, but they don't care."

"I understand. I'm in the same situation as you," I say in sympathy.

"Let's get out of here. I feel like going for a walk." He gets up and carefully puts his guitar in its case.

"Sure."

We head toward a nearby park. On the way, he does something that surprises me: he takes a cigarette pack and lighter from his pocket and lights up.

"I didn't know you smoke."

"I just started," he answers tersely.

"Why did you start?"

"Why does anyone start smoking? Stress, I guess."

"You mean like getting married? Why do you have to do what your family tells you?"

"Because I love them, and I don't want to hurt them."

Sammy struggles with the same things I do. "We all love our parents and family," I say. "But if they really love us, then all they should care about is our happiness and not theirs." Inside, I wince at myself for saying this; why don't I listen to my own advice?

"You're right, but what can we do?" Sammy says. "We can't change that, no matter how much we want to."

"Yes, I know. But I don't think you understand what I mean," I say, feeling bold.

He throws the cigarette butt away. "I know what you mean, Ramy. It's a culture thing, our tradition. And anyway, I don't think there's anything wrong with a union between two people who want to have children."

"What I mean is, I don't want to get married either. Ever."

Did I just say that? Now Sammy will know for sure I'm gay. He stops in his tracks and looks at me. "Why not?"

What should I tell him now? My thoughts race as he stares at me. Then he smiles and says, "That's okay. You don't have to tell me if you don't want to."

"No, it's just that ... I don't like commitment." What a lame response, I think.

"That's understandable, especially since you're still young."

"The truth is, Sammy ..." My voice trails off.

"What?" Sammy looks at me, eyebrows raised.

I lean over and kiss him. Oh my god, I have lost my mind. His eyes are wide open when I pull away.

"What was that?" Sammy says, his hands up. I've made a terrible mistake.

"Sorry. I'm sorry ... I didn't mean to."

"That's ..."

"Look, I'm so sorry. It's just—"

All of a sudden, Sammy punches me in the face. "Are you gay?" he yells.

I stagger about with my hand on my cheek. "No, I'm ..." I start to panic.

He punches me again, this time in the nose, which begins to bleed. Then he pushes me to the ground and kicks me in the stomach. I do nothing to protect myself, nothing to defend myself. He continues to kick me, calling me *lotee* all the while.

Finally, I open my eyes; blood pours from my nose, and it feels like a kidney is punctured. But now there is silence. Sammy is gone. A man approaches me as I lay on the ground and asks, "Are you all right, brother?" I can't speak. I am afraid to move.

"You're hurt," he says. "Look, I live walking distance from here. Why don't you come with me so I can take care of you?"

I look carefully at the man and realize that this is the sheikh. He is dressed in a *dishdasha* and has a full beard and moustache. I reach out my hand, and he helps me get up. He continues to hold my hand as he guides me toward his house. I don't speak as I limp along beside him; I don't want him to know who I am.

His wife opens the door as we approach and gives us a confused look. She pulls back when she sees the blood on my face. The sheikh tells her to get some bandages and hot water. I lie back on the couch, and he uses napkins to wipe the blood from my nose and mouth. His wife comes back, and the sheikh gently cleans, then bandages, my wounds. His hands are warm, soothing. I sit up.

"How are you feeling?" he asks.

"I'm better. Sorry to have bothered you."

"No, it's my pleasure. Who did this to you?"

"I don't know," I lie. "Are you ... Sheikh Ammar?"

"Yes, brother, I am. Do you come to the mosque?"

"Sometimes."

"I don't recall meeting you before."

I stand up. "I've troubled you enough," I say. "I should get going."

"No, no, you have to stay for dinner, at least."

"Thanks, but my brother must be worried about me by now."

"I understand, but you haven't told me your name," the sheikh says with a smile.

"It's Hassan," I lie.

"Nice meeting you, Hassan. Although I wish it had been under different circumstances." Sheikh Ammar reaches for my hand and we shake.

"Thanks for everything!" I say, and mean it.

The walk home feels shorter than it is because I am immersed in confusing thoughts. I am crushed by Sammy's outburst and embarrassed by the kindness shown to me by the sheikh, who may have acted differently if he had known my true identity. Mohammed greets me with a barrage of questions when he sees I've been beaten. I tell him I was with a friend. "What friend? What happened, Ramy?" His voice is grave.

I can't look at him. "I fell and hurt myself."

"Don't lie to me!"

I push past him to get to my room. My brother follows, stopping me before I can close the door. "Tell me the truth," he demands.

"I did!"

"Did you fight with someone?"

"No ... no ..." I stare at the floor, hands fisted against my thighs. I begin to shake, tremors running throughout my body. Still, I don't say anything. Finally Mohammed gives up.

"Ramy ... never mind. You get some rest," he says and leaves.

I think my brother must know the truth, but doesn't want to—can't—face it.

Finally, alone and in bed, I cannot sleep. I keep thinking about Sammy. I've ruined our relationship because of a single mistake, a single kiss.

When night becomes morning, I ride to school with Mohammed once again. But I decide to skip class and try to find

Sammy. I look for him first in the band room; he isn't there. I try the cafeteria and then outside, near the benches; no sign of him there, either. Frustrated, I take a taxi to the grocery store where he works, but his boss tells me he didn't come in to work today. Where is he? I need to see him so I can apologize. I don't know what came over me, I'll tell him. I have destroyed our friendship, I'll say. And it's the most important thing in the world to me. But Sammy is nowhere to be found.

When I get home that night, Mohammed surprises me by telling me that we are invited for dinner at Jameela's house again. Immediately, I feel the need to speak to her so that I can confess how I feel about Sammy, to tell her how much I'm hurting. But I know that isn't possible.

"Can't we reschedule it?" I ask.

"No, that wouldn't be the right thing to do," Mohammed says.

"But I don't feel like going today. My face is bruised, and my ribs still hurt."

"We told the family we're coming. It would be rude to cancel. Go get some rest; you'll feel better later."

I give up and go upstairs to my room. Maybe I'll fall asleep and never wake up. I lie on my bed trying to stifle my tears. It's wrong to feel sorry for myself, but I feel like the entire world has turned against me. Seeing Jameela won't make things any better. And if I were to marry her, wouldn't it ruin her future by making her suffer along with me?

I shut my eyes and am drifting off when a voice whispers in my ear, "Hello, Ramy." My eyes snap open to see a little monster—no, a monster wouldn't look as innocent as this creature. It is small and pink and smiles at me. I open my mouth to speak, but before I can say anything, it puts a finger on my lips.

"I'm Angel Gabriel," he says.

I take a deep breath. "I don't believe you," I say. "I don't believe in God and angels."

"Then you're an idiot!" the creature says. "If you don't believe in God, why do you go to Friday prayers?"

"We all do," I respond. "It's tradition."

"If you go to the mosque, it should be because you want to, not because it's tradition."

"Oh, yes, and pray to a God who condemns me? Why would I want to do that?"

"Who says God condemns you?"

"It's pretty clear, what ... whoever you are."

The little creature scoffs. "I told you, my name is Gabriel. And I know what I'm talking about."

"So why are you here?"

Gabriel leans over and kisses me on the lips. "That is from God," he says and laughs.

"What do you mean?" I say, wiping the back of my hand across my mouth.

"God sends you a kiss and invites you to come to the mosque this Friday."

"Why?"

"You know why."

Then I remember my letter to the sheikh. "Does this have anything to do with the colour pink?" I ask.

"Maybe."

The creature grins, then flutters up to the ceiling and disappears. What was that about? I ask myself. As I rub my eyes, I'm certain that this was a dream. But it felt too real.

At Jameela's home that night, we all gather around the dining room table which is covered with heaping plates of food, including *maqluba*, a casserole of fried eggplant and meats; *tashreeb*, a chicken stew; and *fausolia*, a soup of white beans and lamb.

"Jameela cooked everything today," Jameela's mother announces proudly.

"You're so talented, Jameela," Noor says with a smile. Jameela looks at me expectantly. I smile but don't say anything. After dinner, we sit in the living room, drinking tea and eating homemade biscuits. Noor and *Khala* Najwa talk about a man who proposed to Jameela last year.

"He was a good boy," Najwa says. "He came from a good family."

"Why did she refuse him then?" Noor asks.

"He said he was in love with me, but it was all too quick, you know," Jameela says, answering for herself. "Love has to be built and developed. That's what I believe."

I nod. "You're right," I say, but I am still thinking about Sammy.

In mathematics class the next morning, we are given an exam, the last before the final test to determine if we will graduate. With all that has happened, I had completely forgotten about it, so I didn't study. I stare at the questions; my mind is blank. My brain is not working. I cannot remember anything I've learned. Where is Sammy? Why am I here? I am wasting my time.

I get up and storm out the door before the teacher can say anything. As I walk down the hallway, I see Sammy coming toward me. I can't believe my eyes. He stops and stares at me, saying nothing for what seems like eternity. Then he surprises me by asking, "Can we talk?"

"Yes," I say a little too quickly.

We go outside and sit on a bench in silence. I refuse to begin the conversation, since I don't know what to say. Maybe I should begin by apologizing. But then, *he* was the one who beat *me* up.

"Ramy, I'm sorry about what happened," Sammy finally says.

"No, if anyone should be sorry, it's me," I respond. "I shouldn't have done what I did."

"You didn't do anything wrong. I was angry and violent. That's not me. I don't know what happened."

"No, I made a mistake." Why can't I accept his apology?

"All you did was kiss me."

"I know, but it's wrong."

"No, it isn't."

I try not to appear surprised. "What ... what do you mean? I don't understand."

Sammy stares at the ground in front of him.

"Ramy ... I ... I'm gay." He turns to look at me.

At first, I don't know what to do. Then as if it is the most natural thing in the world, I pull him to me and put my arms around him. In spite of Sammy's torment, I feel like flying.

"When you kissed me, I felt bad because I liked it," he says. "I didn't think. I reacted."

All of a sudden, Sammy kisses me. When he pulls away, he says, "The other night, I should've kissed you back."

"Well, you just did, didn't you?" I say.

"I guess I did," he says, smiling.

I can't believe what is happening. My heart is racing. "I never thought this would happen. I would have never guessed that you ..."

"It's so hard here. We cannot speak of it. Homosexuals are not citizens. They're heathens, to most. But they don't know us very well, do they? Maybe when they do, they'll be able to accept us as God should accept us."

"That will never happen, *habibi*," I say. I think about Mohammed and Noor. I'm certain they believe that homosexuality is a disease that needs to be cured. But if Mohammed, my older brother, my father substitute, truly loves me...

"Does your family know?" I ask.

"No, and they never will." Sammy looks at me gravely.

I nod. "My brother and his wife are the same. They tell us that we should marry women and have children like everyone else. Our religion condemns homosexuality. Allah sends the *lotees* to hell. This is what has been drummed into our heads."

"If you had to choose right now between family and marriage and the one you love, which would you choose?" Sammy asks.

I don't respond. I can't.

"We have to be hypocrites, don't we?" He looks at me, shakes his head sadly, then perks up. "Come to my house, Ramy. We can talk. Maybe you can stay for dinner?"

"What about your mother and sister?"

"It's no big deal. You're my friend."

"All right."

"Good," he says, then grins.

We arrive at Sammy's apartment in Al-Sa'adoon. As soon as he opens the door, I hear his mother yell, "Sammy, are you home?"

We enter the living room together. "Hello, Mother. Remember Ramy?"

"Yes. I do." She says hello, but looks at me as if I'm an insect she'd like to squash. Does she know?

"Ramy is going to stay for dinner. Okay?"

She doesn't respond. "Come see my room," Sammy says to me.

His room is very basic; a bed, a desk, and not much else. But on the walls are posters of Angelina Jolie and the Spice Girls.

"I love the Spice Girls. They're awesome. And Britney, too," he says, grinning.

"Where's your computer?" I ask, looking around.

"I don't have one."

"Why not?"

"I don't see the point. All I need is my guitar." He picks it up and begins to play a few notes.

"I wish I could play an instrument," I say. "You're an amazing guitarist."

Suddenly he puts the guitar down and pulls me into his arms. He kisses me, but this time he lingers, then nudges me onto the bed. I quickly glance at the door to make sure it's locked. What about his mother? Before I know it, Sammy is caressing me gently as he slides himself into me. Beads of perspiration form on my forehead. Lost in the moment, I reach a hand between my own legs.

Sabah al-khair. It is Friday morning. I had no sleep last night. I am only awake because I've had three cups of coffee. Taking my seat on the king's chair before prayers, I look about at the mosque's walls, on which the names of Allah and our prophet are spelled out. Many men and their children are gathered before me, waiting for me to speak. The women upstairs are also waiting. I see Abaddon; her cold eyes are filled with hate.

"*As-salamu alaykum,*" I intone.

Everyone replies in a unified voice: "*Wa-alaykum-as-salaam.*"

I clear my throat, open my notebook, and put on my glasses.

"My dear brothers and sisters, I've had requests from many of you to continue our discussion of Islam and homosexuality. So I have prepared another small lecture to further explore this problem." I pick up the cup of water on the small table in front of me and take a sip.

"My dear brothers and sisters, I think it is obvious that homosexuality is unlawful in Islam. It is neither accepted by the state nor by Islamic society. The Qur'an clearly says that it is unjust, unnatural, a transgression; it is criminal and corrupt." I look over the verses from the Qur'an that condemn homosexuality. They are the same quotes I used the last time. But I will read them aloud again.

"The holy scripture tells us: 'If two men among you commit indecency, punish them both. If they repent and mend their ways, let them be. God is forgiving and merciful.' The problem with the Holy Qur'an is that it doesn't specify what kind of indecency these two men might commit. It doesn't say whether it is with one another or with others. It is vague, but I believe that Allah means two men having sexual relations with one another. And that is *haram*."

I awaken to a sweet kiss from Sammy. He reaches a hand inside my shirt.

"The Qur'an clearly condemns homosexuality, doesn't it? It is there in black and white—and pink—my brothers and sisters. Don't believe otherwise."

I kiss Sammy back, our mouths joined.

"'You lust after men instead of women. Truly, you are a degenerate people,' the Qur'an tells us."

Sammy and I spend the early hours in each other's arms. Morning has never felt so wonderful.

"Do you commit indecency with your eyes open, lustfully seeking men instead of women? Surely you are an ignorant people."

"I think I should go home now," I quietly say to Sammy. "I was supposed to go to Friday prayers with Mohammed. He'll be furious with me."

I glance around; my audience is obviously uncomfortable. "Does anyone have any questions? Any concerns?"
 The mosque is silent. No one moves or makes a sound.

It seems as though there are no questions. But eventually one man raises his hand and asks, "If we know someone is homosexual, do we kill them?"

I pause for a moment, searching for the right answer. "Let God be the judge. If they deserve punishment, it would be for God to decide."

I arrive home, knowing that Mohammed is in the kitchen waiting for me. He is indeed sitting at the table, fingering his prayer beads and praying quietly.

"Where were you?" he asks.

"I was studying at my friend's house," I lie. He puts the beads on the table and looks at me suspiciously.

"Is that right? I saw your mathematics professor yesterday afternoon. He told me you did well on your exam." Mohammed is being sarcastic. "Where were you last night, Ramy?" he persists.

"I told you, I was studying at my friend's."

"Who's your friend?"

"His name is Sammy. He goes to school with me." I begin to walk away; I don't need this confrontation right now.

"And you missed Friday prayers."

"I'm sorry. It won't happen again."

"Aren't you curious what today's lecture was about?" Then suddenly I remember my strange visitor, who had implored me to go. Oh no! "Sheikh Ammar talked about homosexuality."

"Did he?" Now I'm afraid. And curious.

"The topic disgusts me. What do you think?"

"It's contrary to the Qur'an," I say.

He shakes his head. "Never mind. Don't forget that tonight we're going to Jameela's house."

"But we were just there."

"Yes, and we're going again tonight."

"But why?"

He smiles and puts an arm around my shoulder. "Because you are going to propose to her."

My heart starts to race. "But—why so soon? I barely know her."

"You've met with her a few times now. Noor and I think you are ready."

"But I still have two more months until I graduate."

"Well, if you pass and graduate, then we'll have you two married in no time. It'll make Baba and Mama very happy."

"I'm not ready."

"Ramy, you don't understand. If we wait too long, someone else might propose to Jameela."

I nod and sigh. I don't have the strength to fight him right now. "Okay, Mohammed. Whatever you say."

I slump to my room. There I imagine Sammy lying on the bed waiting for me. I fight back the tears, then turn around and head downstairs right past Mohammed.

"Where are you going?" he asks, but I don't respond.

I have decided to see Sheikh Ammar. I cannot wait any longer. I need to know if he is willing to help me. By the time I arrive at his house, I'm breathless with anticipation. I knock on the door and the sheikh's young son answers.

"*As-salamu alaykum*. Is Sheikh Ammar at home?" Ammar comes to the door and nudges his son to the side.

"*Wa-alaykum-as-salaam*, Hassan," he greets me. "Your wounds have already healed."

"I came for tea, sir, if that's okay with you."

"Of course. You are more than welcome anytime."

I smile and follow him into the house. He leads me to the living room, where I sit down on a couch. I look around and feel intimidated by the drawings and paintings of faith all around me.

Sheikh Ammar takes a seat facing me. "I was hoping to see you today at the Friday prayers," he says, hands folded in his lap.

"Sorry, I couldn't come. I had family issues."

"I hope that all your issues have been resolved," he replies benevolently.

If only it were that easy.

The sheikh's wife appears bearing a tray of tea cups and a plate of biscuits. She is wearing a *hejab* and her face is free of makeup. Is this life my fate? I think. She sets the tray on the table without a word and just as quietly leaves.

"What brings you here today?" the sheikh prods.

Before I can respond, his son enters. The sheikh turns to him and says, "Can you excuse us please, Jaffar?" I'm impressed that Ammar treats his son respectfully, like an adult. Mohammed still treats me like a child, always talking down to me. I sense genuine warmth in Sheikh Ammar, an easiness that encourages me to be honest with him.

"I want to confess something," I tell him.

He puts his hands up. "Before you go on, I want to assure you that you are free to say anything. I am not your father. Or even your brother Mohammed."

"How do you know my brother?"

"He comes to prayers frequently. He's one of the more dedicated members. It's obvious you are brothers."

I sigh. "So you know my name isn't Hassan."

He grins. "I know," he says.

"But how? Did Mohammed tell you?"

"No. I just know. What *is* your name, brother?" he asks.

"Ramy."

"That's a beautiful name. But Hassan is even more beautiful. It is the name of Imam Ali's son." He smiles.

"And I want to tell you something else," I say hesitantly.

"You're not Ramy either?"

His humour makes me smile. "I want to say ..." I can't find the words; this is more difficult than I thought it would be. I finally blurt out, "Pink."

Sheikh Ammar's eyes widen as he silently stares at me.

Shinoo? What? Sooner or later, I expected to meet the writer of that letter. But I do not want to help this young man. I look up and see Gabriel near the ceiling, wings fluttering, looking on with approval, as if I have just achieved something great. What am I to say? Gabriel is no help. I pick up my teacup and begin sipping. Ramy does the same.

God forgive me. I feel claustrophobic and begin to sweat.

"Are you all right, Sheikh?" the young man asks.

I reach for a napkin to wipe the sweat from my brow. "Yes, I'm fine. I'm sorry, what were you saying?"

He pauses for a moment, then tells me that he was the one who wrote the letter and that he needs my help. But how can I help a homosexual man? I must follow God's words in the Qur'an, the holiest book.

"Exactly how can I help you?" I finally ask.

"I don't know," he says despondently, then stares at the floor.

I sit back on the couch and sigh. I was afraid this would happen. The sheikh doesn't appear to have any desire to help me. I look at him; he is silent and appears to be deep in thought. Then I realize that he's fighting a battle too, a war between his heart, his mind, and his soul. Not unlike Sammy and me. But I think his struggle must pose a further dilemma: a part of him wants to help me, yet he feels he must obey God and the Qur'an.

"So, are you going to help me?" I challenge, returning to the subject at hand.

"I'm not sure how I can help someone who is homosexual," he says.

His words hurt me, but who else can I turn to?

"My suggestion ... is to try to resist it and get married and have a family," he says.

I feel panicky. I thought the sheikh would have more compassion.

"But I won't be happy and neither will my wife," I say.

We both hear a shuffling noise and turn toward it. Ammar's son has been standing in the doorway, listening. "Jaffar! Go to your room!" the sheikh shouts. The boy scurries away.

"If you're not willing to change, how can I help you?" Ammar continues.

"Why do I need to change?"

"It's simple. God damns the *lotees*. Haven't you read the Qur'an?"

"I've read the Qur'an, and I know the passages you're referring to. None of them clearly condemns homosexuality."

"But these are the words of God."

"No," I say. "People misinterpret the words to suit their beliefs." I can't believe my own audacity. How dare I challenge a holy man? The sheikh gets up and grabs the Qur'an from a nearby table. He flips through several pages and stops. "God says in the Qur'an, 'We also sent Lot.' He said to his people: 'Do ye commit lewdness such as no people in creation ever committed before you? For ye practice your lusts on men in preference to women: ye are indeed a people transgressing beyond bounds.' I assume you have heard the story of Lot."

"Yes, I have."

"You can find it in the Hebrew scriptures too. And in the bibles of Christianity."

"I thought the people of Lot were punished for adultery, not specifically for homosexuality."

"Weren't you listening? God clearly states it was for having preferences for men instead of women."

"Wasn't Lot's wife punished, too? She wasn't a man, was she?" I challenge.

"Yes, but—"

"So they weren't punished simply for their so-called homosexuality."

He is quiet for a moment, then says, "There's a quote from Prophet Muhammed, peace be upon him, that says, 'When a man mounts another man, the throne of God shakes.'"

"I don't believe that. I've heard that many of the Hadiths of the Prophet were made up by radicals who hated homosexuals."

"You're not willing to listen, are you? Your eyes and ears are closed to the words of God." Sheikh Ammar shakes his head, clearly frustrated with me. He's just like the rest of them. He spouts what he's been taught without question. In school, they taught us critical thinking. What good is it here?

"What about me, then?" I ask.

"I told you, change your ways."

"But I can't! I was born this way!"

He smiles at me benevolently. "Nobody is born that way," he says.

"You're just like them," I mutter.

"When a majority of people believes in a similar ideology, it might have some truth to it."

"But if God made me and all others like me ..."

"I don't know what to say to that. You'll have to ask Him on Judgment Day."

"Why bother? We *lotees* are going to hell, aren't we?" My emotions are starting to take over. Stand your ground, I tell myself.

"Look, God is most merciful. You can still change, and I'm sure He will open a new page with you."

"You want me to turn myself into someone I'm not. It is not easy."

"Why not? People can change."

"Yes. And I've struggled my whole life, trying to change. But I now know that I am who I am. I can't do it anymore."

"So you've given up?"

"No, it's not that—"

"Then what?"

I pause. "God made me this way. Since the day I was born, I was different. But you and everyone else around me won't see it."

"And you don't understand that westerners are obsessed with perversions such as homosexuality, adultery, material wealth, and other filth."

I laugh.

"What's so funny?" he says indignantly.

"You're blaming it on westerners now?"

"Ever since America invaded our country, we hear more and more about sex, nudity, superficial values. And yes, *lotees*. Before, these things didn't exist here."

"Why can't you see it as freedom?" I look up at the doorway. His son is again standing there, not quite out of sight.

The sheikh chuckles. "Brother, everyone is free to do whatever they want. You can sleep with a cow behind closed doors and no one will know. Except God, of course. He is all-knowing and all-seeing. Islam is here to guide you to the right path."

"I know, I know. It's all about the right path, the afterlife. But what about here and now? How can I marry a woman knowing we will both be miserable for the rest of our lives?"

"But you haven't even tried. You might find you like being married and raising a family."

I haven't tried. But why should I, when I know it isn't right? "Look, I need your help ..." I'm tired of arguing with him.

"I'm trying to help you, Ramy, but you're not listening."

"But what you're telling me is no help at all." I fight back the tears.

As Ammar reaches for a biscuit, he catches sight of his son. "Jaffar! Didn't I tell you to go to your room?"

"Baba, I ..." Jaffar says as he takes a few steps forward.

"Go to your room!" the sheikh bellows. The boy runs down the hall.

"Is this conversation going anywhere?" the sheikh asks.

I take a deep breath. "Sir, this is my final question to you: why can't I be a devout Muslim and be true to myself at the same time?"

"Because being devout isn't simply about praying. It's also

about abiding by the Qur'an and fulfilling God's requirements."

"But who says the Qur'an tells us God's requirements?"

"Are you questioning the Qur'an now?" Sheikh Ammar's face is turning a deep red.

I've gone too far. I get up, nod to the sheikh, and leave.

When Ramy is gone, I am relieved. It feels like I've lost a year from my life. I sit back on the couch and sigh, exhausted. He wants my help but refuses it. He does not seem to understand that homosexuality is wrong. And Ramy wants to pray to God when he is committing the worst sin of all.

"Ammar, what happened?" Shams asks. Without her *hejab* now, she is seated on the couch across from me where Ramy had been. "Why was that man so unhappy when he left?"

"Were you listening?"

"No. But he looked as though he had the weight of the world on his shoulders when he walked out."

"Never mind. Forget about him. He just needed some help."

"But you didn't help him, did you?"

"No," I say, sighing again. "I think this man is lost. He doesn't know who he is. He just needs to reach out to God and He will help him."

"Can you not help him, *habibi*? God will reward you. I just know it."

"Baba, I'm sorry," Jaffar's voice intrudes.

I sit up quickly and say, "How many times have I told you to go to your room?"

"What did that man want from you?"

"Go to your room, I say." I am not in the mood; my thoughts are muddled.

Jaffar leaves. I have hurt my son, the son whom I love with all my heart and soul. I lie back again on the couch, trying to rest. But I am haunted by Ramy's words. How can I make him understand that homo-sexuality is forbidden?

"You can't!" a voice intrudes again. I open my eyes; Gabriel flutters around me.

"I didn't know that mindreading was a skill of yours," I respond.

"You've made a mistake."

"Maybe in your eyes, but God will thank me for this later."

"You refused to help that young man!"

"I didn't refuse to help him," I say angrily. "He refused to listen."

"And you are always right."

Abaddon appears across from Gabriel. She glares at him, saying, "Don't try to persuade him otherwise. He's on the right path."

"Are you going to let Abaddon control you?" Gabriel asks.

"Of course not. I make my own decisions."

"Ramy needed your help," Gabriel says. "He wanted to find a way to balance his religion and his sexuality. A way to live contentedly with both."

"That can't be done. You're either a devout Muslim or you're not," Abaddon says.

Gabriel points a finger at her. "What do you know? Just go away. I'm talking to Ammar."

"Ammar, don't listen to Gabriel. He's homosexual himself." Abbadon has a smirk on her face.

Gabriel slaps Abaddon with a wing. Her burka hides her reaction. Then she begins to laugh.

"She is a fake and a liar, Ammar. Don't listen to her!" Gabriel flaps his wings in emphasis.

"I don't want to listen to either of you. Just leave me alone!" I plead.

"No, I will never leave you alone." Gabriel leans over and kisses me on the lips.

Suddenly I am transported to a room I've never seen before, in the presence of a beautiful young man. His hands are tied to the bedposts, and he is naked. I try to close my eyes, but can't. I try to back away, but something pushes me toward him.

"What are you doing, Gabriel? Let me go!" I call out.

The young man says something in Hebrew that I don't understand. I realize he is one of the men of Lot. Still trying to back away, I am forced to move closer and closer to him.

"Let me go, Gabriel!" I shriek.

I look down; I am naked now too. I try to cover my genitals, but my hands won't move. My penis is stirring; I try to calm it. Suddenly, I'm pressing against the young man and entering him; he whimpers. After a few thrusts, I feel the need to cum. I have never felt this before in my life, not even with Shams. I close my eyes, trying to steady my breathing. When I open them, I am back home, with Gabriel hovering nearby.

"Did you enjoy it?" he asks.

"No!"

Gabriel chuckles. "I know you did," he says.

I sit on my bed and imagine Jameela next to me. She looks at me expectantly. I'm not sure what to say or do. Should I help her take her clothes off? Does she want me to kiss her on the lips? She wouldn't be asking for too much; I could pretend ... But how can you pretend to love someone, to feign passion when it isn't there?

A knock on the door disturbs my thoughts. "Come in," I say.

Noor has a smile on her face. "Are you ready for tonight?"

Right. I am so ready. I can't wait to see the woman of my life, the one I'm going to marry and make babies with. "Yes," I sigh.

"What are you going to wear?"

"The suit that Mohammed lent me the last time, I guess."

"No, no." She thinks for a second. "I'll take you shopping for a new one."

"What's the point? You'd be wasting your money."

"You don't understand. This is a very special day for all of us. My son is getting engaged!" I am her son on a day like this.

The two of us take a taxi to the local market area, close to where Sammy works. I want to go find him, but now I am at Noor's mercy. Everything is cheap here—grocery stores, clothing stores, shops that sell *hejabs*. She and I go into a run-down shop where Mohammed once bought a suit. The owner greets us enthusiastically.

"How is your husband?" he asks. "I haven't seen him in a while."

"He's well. It is close to the end of the school year, so he's busy grading exams," Noor responds.

I have exams of my own coming up, but I haven't been studying. But do I care? No. So many people graduate with useless degrees and cannot find work in the end. The only people able to get good jobs are the children of the wealthy and powerful. I can see where my future is headed—struggling to make a living in a tedious, low-paying government job. We all thought that, after the war, work would be plentiful and wages would increase. We couldn't have been more wrong.

I sit down on a chair as Noor looks for the right colour shirt for me. "What do you think?" she asks, holding up two.

I shrug. "It doesn't matter."

"I'm not the one marrying Jameela, *habibi*. Make up your mind."

The clerk measures me for size. I feel like a doll being played with as he gently pulls and tugs me this way and that. Before too long, I am outfitted with a new suit, shirt, and tie. When I come out of the dressing room, Noor says, "You look so handsome." But all I feel is dread. After making the purchase, Noor and I walk down the street, past a variety of other shops. I look in the direction of the grocery store where Sammy works, then stare ahead. Perhaps the sheikh is right. Perhaps I haven't been trying hard enough.

"Jameela is a good woman," I suddenly say to Noor.

"Yes, she is," Noor responds. "She comes from a good family. I'm sure you two will be happy."

At home, I take a shower and get ready. The time has come, and I feel nervous. As we drive away, I study the exterior of the house, as if this is the last time I will see it. I feel as if I'm on my way to an execution.

When we arrive at Jameela's house, Mohammed and Noor flank me as we walk toward the door. After exchanging pleasantries with Jameela's father, we go inside and wait for Jameela and her mother. Noor, next to me, notices my nervousness. She can't possibly know how miserable I am. I try to hide my misery as she pats my hand.

"You'll be fine. God is with you," she whispers. It feels as if she is turning me over to enemy troops. Snap out of it, I tell myself, it's not that bad. Finally, Jameela and Najwa appear; Jameela is wearing a red and white dress, and her head is covered with a bright white *hejab*. Najwa welcomes us, but I feel as though Jameela's eyes look at me with pity.

Mohammed gets to his feet. "It's our honour and pleasure, sir, to know your family," he says to Ghassan. It is customary to praise and compliment the bride's family on these occasions. After a long preamble, he announces: "My brother, Ramy, wishes to bring our families together."

I do? You know the truth, Mohammed, I think but do not say. "We would be honoured—Ramy would be honoured," Mohammed continues, "to take your daughter's hand in marriage."

I glance over at Jameela, who does not look back at me.

"Thank you for your kind words, sir," her father replies. "My family would be honoured to give our daughter to your brother in marriage."

Noor and Jameela's mother smile at each other and begin to chant *halaheel* in celebration.

"As you know, Ramy will be graduating in a few months," Mohammed says. "Then, if God is willing, they will be married."

Najwa kisses her daughter, who manages a weak smile.

Mohammed pulls me to my feet and hugs me tight. "Congratulations, *habibi*," he says.

I smile but am fighting back tears. Why can't I stand up for myself now, like I did with Sheikh Ammar?

Bismillah Al Rahman Al Raheem. I sit down on the couch, reading the Qur'an, haunted by sinful images that refuse to leave me. I stop reading to pray to God to brush the devil off my shoulders, trying to return to the holy man I present myself to be. But images of being with the beautiful young man flood my mind. I pray to God to take these thoughts away. Closing the Qur'an, I kiss the cover and then go to Jaffar's room.

"Come in," he says when I knock.

I enter, smiling. "What are you doing?"

"Reading the Qur'an, Baba. As is your wish."

I nod. "That's true. But if you don't want to read it now, that's okay too." I reach down and give him a hug. "Jaffar, I wanted to ask you what you heard when that young man was visiting today."

"I didn't hear anything, Baba," he says, not looking at me.

"Jaffar, good Muslims don't lie to their fathers," I admonish. I sit down next to him.

After several moments of silence, he says, "Baba, why is that man homosexual?"

So he did hear our conversation. "Jaffar, he is sinful and dirty and should be ashamed of himself."

"But why?"

"Because God forbids his actions." I recite a relevant verse from the Qur'an and then say, "I don't want you to worry about him. He has made mistakes, and we should pray to God to forgive him and help him to become pure and holy again."

"Okay," Jaffar says.

I kiss my son's forehead and leave his room. Walking down the hallway, I hear sounds coming from my bedroom. It must be Shams. I'm sure she's still awake. She never sleeps until I am in bed next to her. When I get to the room, she is sitting at her dressing table looking into the mirror, putting makeup on her face.

"I thought I'd surprise you," Shams says with a smile.

"Ah," I say, returning the smile. She stands up, kisses me, and nudges me toward the bed. She gets on top of me, her long red hair falling over my face as she kisses me again. She pulls my head toward her chest. I am sweating, my heart is racing. I feel inexplicably frightened, trapped. Shams takes my hand and moves it downward. I am not enjoying this. I suddenly flash on the handsome young man and, before I know it, cum before entering her. She climbs off me, looking disappointed.

I know she wants me to give her pleasure. But I can't. I am a failure as a husband.

I enter the shop. It's the first time I've been in a place like this. A friend told me about it. I look around at the different types of weapons on display, from guns to knives to machetes. Shit, this is terrifying. The shopkeeper, a man a few years older than me with thick facial hair, stands next to the display cabinet. There is no one else in the store.

"Can I help you?" His smile makes me uneasy.

I hesitate. I know I shouldn't be doing this. "I'm looking for a gun ..." I say hesitantly.

"Are you looking for a specific type?"

"No, just a regular one. The cheapest you've got."

Without questioning the reasons for my interest, the shop-keeper unlocks the cabinet and takes out a Cobra CA380.

"How much is it?"

"The price is negotiable," he says, that smile creeping across his face again.

I take a deep breath and pull out a watch that Mohammed once gave me.

"This is all I've got," I say. He takes hold of it and examines it.

"It's a nice watch," he comments.

"I got it as a birthday present."

"Like I care?" he says. The smile is gone now. But he agrees to the exchange, and before long I am out on the sidewalk with the Cobra and some ammunition. I take a deep breath. Do I really want to do this?

Back home, Noor is in the kitchen, cooking. I find Moham-med reading in the living room.

"I need to talk to you," I say.

"What about?"

"You're my older brother, no?" I begin.

He chuckles. "Is this some sort of a joke?"

"Well, are you?"

"Why?"

"How could you do this to me?"

Mohammed gives me a confused look. "What do you mean?" he asks.

"How could you force me to marry Jameela?"

"I want the best for you, Ramy. I know you'll be happy with her."

"You think so? How the hell can you be so sure?"

I put my hand in my pocket and wrap it around the gun. Mohammed sees me fiddling.

"What do you have in there?" he asks.

My body begins to shake. "Don't pretend you've forgotten, Mohammed. How old were you then? Sixteen? I remember that day very well."

"I don't know what you're talking about."

I pull out the gun. Mohammed is startled. I hear Noor gasp from beyond the doorway. "What are you doing, Ramy? Are you crazy?" she cries out.

"All these years, and I didn't say anything ..."

"What are you talking about?"

I aim the gun at Mohammed. "Now I don't care anymore."

"Calm down, Ramy! You're overreacting!"

"Remember what Father did to me? You knew all along but didn't say anything. I remember telling you about it, but you said to keep quiet for the love of Allah."

I point the gun at Mohammed's head. He throws his arms up in the air.

"And now you want me to get married? How can

I marry Jameela when I'm not even attracted to her? Or any other woman, for that matter."

"Ramy, look, he never touched you. I swear."

"You're lying!"

"I'm sorry you think that, Ramy, but I'm not lying. Look, if you need to see a doctor, I'll take you tomorrow. Just don't do anything stupid."

I put my finger on the trigger. Mohammed shuts his eyes; Noor screams. I lift the gun and aim it at him, then pull the trigger. The shot is loud, and I'm momentarily stunned. "I'm fucking gay, Mohammed!" I scream.

The words echo in my head when I wake up. Have I shouted them out loud? It was a horrifying dream.

I open the drawer of my night table and take out the watch that Mohammed gave me for my sixteenth birthday; a gift, too, for my silence. When he gave it to me, he said, "When your son grows up, pass this on to him." I wrap both hands around the watch and hold it close to my heart.

It is a few nights later. The sky is coal-black, brightened by flickering stars that look down at Sammy and me as I rest in his arms. We are standing outside the car, staring at a full moon; its beauty and tranquility belie this violent, narrow-minded country. Too many people here are blinded by tradition, bent on maintaining the status quo, and upholding the word of Allah. Iraq could be a place of beauty too, if only its heart weren't so corrupted.

"The moon looks so free," I tell Sammy. "No one tells it what to do."

"Yes, but even the moon is restricted by routine. It repeats its cycle over and over again. It never dies."

"You're right. Immortality doesn't bring happiness. We mortals need to stick together."

He kisses me. I feel guilty for not telling Sammy the truth. I know I should tell him about my engagement with Jameela, but I cannot. I take a deep breath.

"I wish we could run away together somewhere," I say.

"Sure. I mean, wouldn't we all rather live somewhere else? A better country?"

"Somewhere like Turkey. Or America." Suddenly I don't feel so despondent. Tell him the truth, Ramy, I tell myself. You can't put it off forever.

"Sammy ... there is something I have to tell you."

He looks at me. "What's wrong?"

"Sammy ... I'm engaged now."

"What?"

"I'm engaged. To a woman."

Then I tell him the whole story from beginning to end, my heart aching more with each word. When I'm done, I look into Sammy's eyes and see anger, but mostly hurt. Mostly hurt.

"So what are you going to do?" he asks.

"I don't know. I don't love her. I know I'm going to make her life miserable."

"Why didn't you tell your brother the truth?"

"That I'm gay? I can't!"

"No, I mean you should have told Mohammed that you don't like Jameela."

"But then he'd just find someone else for me, Sammy. I need your help. I don't know what to do."

"What about us?"

"That's why I'm telling you this. I want to be with you for the rest of my life."

"But you don't really know me ..." His voice trails off.

"What are you talking about?"

"I mean, do you really know me?"

"Sammy, of course. I know you. Like, inside and out."

"What I'm trying to tell you, Ramy ..." He pauses, takes a deep breath. "What I'm saying is, I can't wait for you."

"What do you mean?"

"You have a fiancée now. You just have to accept it."

I can't believe what I'm hearing. "What's that supposed to mean? So you're not going to fight for me?"

"What do you want me to do?"

I hesitate. I don't really know. I was hoping that *he'd* know what to do. But now Sammy is turning his back on me, when I need him the most.

"Sammy, I need you. We can't just say goodbye and that's that."

"You know I can't come between you and your future wife."

"But I don't want to be with her."

"Yeah, you've made that clear."

"And I don't want to lose my brother either."

"Look, Ramy, we all have to make sacrifices in life. You can't have it all."

"But why can't I have both you and Jameela?" But even I know how ridiculous this sounds.

"Ramy, you have to understand my situation. I can't come between you and Jameela. If you choose to marry her, you have to live with the consequences."

I feel broken right now. Incomplete.

"Sammy, please."

"Eventually you'll move on and forget about me." How can he be so cold?

"I'll never forget about you," I sob.

When he drops me off at home, I look at him long and hard. I don't ever want to forget his face. Then, without a word, I get out of the car.

Mohammed is up, seated at the kitchen table waiting for me. When he asks yet again, "Where were you?" I tell him I was at a friend's house. Whether he believes me or not, I don't care.

In my room, I lie on the bed and cry until there are no tears left. The next morning, I ignore Mohammed as he repeatedly knocks on the door, yelling, "Wake up, Ramy."

"I'm sick," I finally reply.

"What's wrong?" he asks. "Look, open the door."

"I'm sick. Please, Mohammed, just let me rest."

I put a pillow over my head and pretend to fall back to sleep. After a while, he finally gives up.

A little later, I hear Noor's whispery voice at the door. "Ramy, it's me." I get up and open it and she walks in with a tray of food. "I thought you might want to eat."

"I'm not really hungry, Noor."

She sits on the bed next to me. "What's wrong, *habibi*? You can tell me anything."

"I swear nothing is wrong, Noor. I'm fine." I turn my head to face the wall.

"Is it about the engagement?"

I pause before saying, "No."

"Look at me, Ramy." I turn around. "I only want happiness for you. If you're not happy about something, tell me, and I will help you."

I fall into her arms. "I love you so much," I say. Still, despite her kindness, I cannot bring myself to tell her the truth.

Ya rab. I wake up early today and feel refreshed. In the kitchen, I drink a glass of milk and eat an egg sandwich. Then I return to my room. Shams is beginning to stir. She opens her eyes and sees me, but she looks away; she is ashamed of what happened last night. But she will forget about it, I tell myself, and move on.

I leave the house and take a taxi to Ramy's; I've already gotten his address by asking at the mosque. His brother is coming out as I arrive, on his way to work. He seems ecstatic to see me.

"What a surprise! How are you, Sheikh Ammar? How's your family?"

"Great, thank you."

"What brings you here today?"

"I came to see your brother. Is he home?"

"Yes, he is ..." A look of concern comes across Mohammed's face. "What has he done?" he asks. "What trouble has he caused?"

"No, nothing of the sort," I say. "You go on to work. I just want to speak with him."

"This is the first time you've visited my house. I must welcome you properly."

"No, no. You're going to be late, brother."

Mohammed sighs. "All right," he says, looking reluctant to leave. He must be a little suspicious. I assume that Ramy hasn't told Mohammed his secret. I don't blame him; Mohammed might do something rash. After all, I remember what Mohammed asked at the mosque.

I knock on the door and a woman answers. I assume she is Mohammed's wife.

"*As-salamu alaykum,* sister," I greet her.

"*Wa-alaykum-as-salaam.*"

"May I have a word with Ramy?"

"He'll be coming down in a few minutes. Won't you come inside?"

I nod and she leads me into the living room before repairing to the kitchen. I am looking at family photographs on the wall when Ramy comes bounding down the stairs.

"What a surprise," he says.

"*Wa-alaykum-as-salaam.* Is this how you greet a guest? Where are your manners?"

"No, it's just that … I didn't expect to see you here."

"I came to have a chat with you. But maybe it's not such a good idea to talk here."

"Why not?"

"Because the topic of our conversation might not be appropriate for others to hear."

Ramy closes the living room door, then sits down across from me. "So, what do you want?"

"Ramy, I first want to apologize to you for my behaviour the last time we met."

I wonder what has caused such a drastic change in Sheikh Ammar.

"I really wanted to help you, yet I couldn't," he tells me.

"And now you can help me?" I don't trust him; he must see that.

"I can try."

"How?"

"I don't know." He looks troubled.

"What is it, Sheikh Ammar? You came to talk to me, so go ahead."

"I felt bad because I dismissed you so hastily. I didn't take the time to even consider a possible solution to your problem. I shouldn't have done that."

"Why the sudden change?" I ask angrily and get up.

"What do you mean?"

I turn and glare at him.

"May I have a glass of water?" he asks. Without replying, I retreat to the kitchen.

Ramy is confused; I don't blame him. I am known for being consistent in my beliefs, for being strong and solid. I don't understand what's happening to me either. But in some small way, it feels good; I want to embrace it.

Ramy returns and hands me a glass of water, then sits on the couch across from me again.

"Did I tell you I'm engaged now?" he says with a smirk.

Sheikh Ammar mutters his congratulations without looking at me. There is something different about him. But what?

"You are looking forward to your marriage?" he asks.

"No. I'm only doing it to make Mohammed and Noor happy."

"And what would make you happy?"

I think about it for a moment. "Going to America," I say. "But that's a hopeless dream. I'd love to see the Statue of Liberty in person."

"A statue is a statue. How can it give you freedom if it's just an object? You shouldn't depend on an object for freedom. You have to find freedom within yourself."

"It's impossible to find freedom in this shitty country," I reply, the anger palpable in my throat. I think of Sammy and our last kiss. "I don't want to live here anymore. I don't want to get married or have children. But what can I do?"

"Ramy, you want to live in a perfect world," the sheikh says. "I don't think such a place exists."

Maybe he's right. But I want to live somewhere I can be free to love another man. "I want to live my life," I say.

"America is not as free as you think it is. And do you know anyone there?"

"No."

Sheikh Ammar sighs. "You can't live your life like this," he says. "You must pray to Allah for forgiveness. You have to ask Him for help. What I want to tell you is that you can change."

"How can I change?"

"You must supress these feelings that you have. I suggest you get married. This... this will be better for you."

"What's the point of lying to yourself and lying to your wife and children?"

Sheikh Ammar's face goes pale. "*Ya Allah*. Brother, you can't do this."

I stand up to shake hands with Sheikh Ammar; he suddenly kisses me on the cheek, mere millimetres from my lips. What has just happened?

"I'm sorry," he says and leaves the house quickly.

In the afternoon, I take a taxi to the university to look for Sammy. The thought of never seeing him again is unbearable. Wandering through the halls, I bump into Mohammed. He gives me a surprised look. "I thought you were sick!"

"I came to do some studying," I say, even though I don't have my books with me. Mohammed is not stupid, and I should know better than to try to lie to him. Habit, I guess.

"Your exams are coming up, you know," he says sternly.

"I know, I know. I'm studying very hard." But now that I think about it, do I even want to pass? I mean, if I do and get my degree, I'll have no excuse to keep from marrying.

"What did Sheikh Ammar want?" he asks.

"He wanted to know why I haven't been attending prayers," I lie. "He's asking others too; I was on a list."

"What did you say?"

"I told him I've been nervous about my upcoming marriage."

"I hope he wasn't angry," Mohammed says. "I'm going home. Do you want a ride?"

"I'm going to stay and study."

"Okay, suit yourself," he says, then leaves.

I sigh in relief and continue my search for Sammy. Although if I find him, I'm not sure of what I might say.

Astaghfirullah. What have I done? How could I do this to myself, to my family? Shame, shame on you, Ammar. How can I go home now? I can't face anyone. I walk down the street despondent, feeling dirty. I am a sheikh, a holy man, yet I am worse than a criminal. What is happening to me? He is so young, so troubled. He was seeking my strength, my knowledge and guidance. And I ...

I knock on the door and Sammy's mother answers it.

"Hello, *khala*. Is Sammy home?"

"Yes, he is," she answers sternly. I'm relieved to hear that he's home. She leads me inside without a word; it's obvious she still doesn't like me. What has Sammy told her about me? I find him in his room; he looks at me sternly too. "What are you doing here?" he asks.

"I need to talk to you," I answer.

"I thought I made it clear. It's over."

"It's not over for me."

He grabs my arm. "Are you crazy? Why are you here?" he says, then storms out of the room toward the front door. I follow him outside.

"Sammy, wait! I need you."

"Stop it! My mother will hear you."

"I love you, Sammy." My voice sounds plaintive, even to me. I step closer to kiss him, but he pushes me away.

"What are you doing? People will see."

His beautiful hazel eyes are filled with anger. He turns and marches back inside. I am shattered.

Drowning in an ocean of guilt, I shiver. I am standing at the door of my house holding the doorknob, too weak to open it. I struggle to speak.

Shams opens the door. "Ammar," she gasps. "What's wrong?" She takes my arm and pulls me inside, locking the door behind us.

"I'm cold."

She leads me to our bed and covers me with several blankets.

"*Bardan*," I say. I'm so cold.

"I know, *habibi*."

Jaffar comes in, takes my hand and kisses it. "Are you all right, Baba?"

I pat his hand to reassure him. Shams leans over and kisses me on the forehead.

Mohammed insists that I visit Jameela. He tells me that I should see my fiancée every day and get to know her better. But I have no desire for that. I only do it because I have no choice.

At the dinner table with Jameela and her parents, I smile and nod at the appropriate times. Her parents do most of the talking. Jameela notices how quiet I am and remains quiet herself. After dinner, her parents leave us alone to sit in the living room and drink tea.

"I want to show you what I've been working on," she tells me.

She gets up and leaves the room. Moments later, she returns with a painting that looks unfinished. I see different shades of pink representing incomplete shapes.

"Why did you choose pink?"

"Pink is the colour of love and affection. It's one of my favourite colours."

I nod but don't say anything.

"Why are you always so quiet?" she asks.

"Jameela, tell me something. You were engaged to that other man. Why did you choose me and not him?" I say, ignoring her question.

She pauses, then says, "I think ... because you're a work in progress."

Ya Rab saa'dny. Ya Rab ehdeny. God, please help me. I haven't stopped shivering, despite being smothered by many layers of blankets. Shams has been putting wet cloths on my forehead, an old tradition that many think cures a fever. It hasn't worked so far.

"What happened?" she asks as she combs my damp hair.

"Nothing," I mutter. I find it difficult to keep my teeth from chattering. All of a sudden I see Abaddon at the foot of the bed, a cunning grin on her face.

"I'll heat up some more water," Shams says. When she leaves, Abaddon comes closer.

"You never listen to my advice, and now you're going to hell," Abaddon says. She sits on the edge of the bed beside me. "When you kiss me, I don't feel any love," she complains, leaning closer. "You are a hypocrite."

Her face is covered by a burka. She slowly removes it, and I realize that Abaddon is my wife.

In class, other students are poring over the exam like they know what they're doing. I try my best, but it feels hopeless. I am certain I will fail it. Perhaps it is for the best; at least then I might not have to marry Jameela.

When the exam is over, I walk past the band room again to see if Sammy is there. But then I realize that it no longer matters; he doesn't want to see me anymore. Why should I care for him? But I stand outside the empty room, wishing that things were different.

"Ramy."

The voice surprises me; my heart starts to race. I turn and see Sammy.

He touches my arm gently. "Can we talk?"

Ya Rab saa'dny. I sit up in bed; I'm no longer shivering. Shams sits next to me, caressing my arm with her soft fingers.

"Can you leave me alone? I need time to think," I tell her.

"You need me by your side, Ammar."

"I know. Just a few minutes please, darling."

She nods and leaves the room. I get up and lock the door, then go to my wife's dressing table.

Sammy and I walk past the benches toward the trees. When I'm with him, the time, the place, even I myself seem to disappear. I can only see, feel, smell Sammy.

"What do we do now, Ramy?"

I sigh, not knowing what to say. I remember when Ali and I were in a similar situation. We wanted to be together, but couldn't.

"You know, Sammy, if I could choose between you and Jameela, I'd pick you in a minute. Honestly, you mean everything to me."

"If you marry Jameela, I can't be with you."

"I don't want to be with her." Even to me, my voice sounds whiny, childish.

"Come here," he says and pulls me into his arms. Glancing around quickly to make sure no one can see us, he puts his lips on mine. I feel alive again.

Allah hates the *lotees*. I take off my clothes and look into the mirror. *Shino hatha al jamal*. There is hair everywhere on my body; it disgusts me. I don't recognize the person in the mirror. What in God's name is happening to me? Suddenly, there is a knock at the door, and Shams' voice calls my name.

"Yes, *habibti*?"

"Sheikh Jassem is here to see you." He is the leader of the neighbourhood mosque. My mosque.

"What does he want from me?"

"I don't know. He's waiting in the living room."

I groan, quickly put my clothes back on, and head for the living room. Sheikh Jassem is dressed in the traditional *dishdasha*, a smile on his bearded face. He has grown old since I last saw him.

"*As-salamu alaykum*, brother Ammar," he greets me.

I return the salaams and shake his hand. He looks perplexed. Did he expect me to kiss him on the cheek, too?

"Sit down, Jassem," I say. "Would you like tea?"

"No, thank you, brother. I have business to attend to."

"Then why are you here?" He seems surprised by my bluntness.

"Brother Ammar, is something wrong?" His voice is filled with concern.

"What do you mean? I'm perfectly fine. Why would you think there's something wrong?"

"Then why haven't you been attending the mosque?"

"Because ... I am retiring," I blurt out.

Sheikh Jassem's eyes widen. "Retiring? Why, brother?"

"I'm getting old, and I want to rest."

"No, no. You have so many years left," Jassem says. He is twenty years older than me, but youthful and full of energy.

"Brother, I cannot do it anymore," I respond. And it's true. I cannot bear the thought. It's time for me to retire.

"But why? Has something happened?" I have no answer, at least none that would satisfy him. Finally, without saying anything, he nods and leaves. I know I have disappointed him, but I cannot be a holy man now, cannot see a way to reconcile my new feelings with Islam. It can't be done.

Shams comes in and looks at me sternly.

"What?" I ask.

"Is it true what I just heard?"

"Yes, it's true."

"If you're retiring, how are we going to live?"

That hasn't crossed my mind. How is my family going to live, indeed?

Sammy and I are driving in the middle of the night. He has one hand on the wheel as he holds his arm around me, and I feel safe. I don't need anyone else, just him. I take his hand and kiss it.

We see a checkpoint ahead and both of us sit up. During Saddam's reign, we had no checkpoints, but now there are too many of them. There are Sunni and Shia areas, a distinction we didn't have before. It is a sad situation. Before the war, we were all Iraqis. Mohammed is Sunni and Noor is Shia, yet they reconciled their differences and got married because they loved each other. I don't know whether Sammy is Sunni or Shia, and I don't care.

Two officers approach us and ask for Sammy's identification card. He pulls it out of his wallet and hands it the officer, who is about the same age as us. Since the war, people have become savages, and for what? We say we have freedom, but it is more like the worst kind of anarchy. Theft, murders, torture—and they call us criminals for our sexuality.

The officer looks at Sammy. "Are you Sunni or Shia?" he asks.

"Both."

"Explain."

"My mother is Shia. My father is Sunni."

The officer turns to me. "And you?"

"I'm both, too."

He returns to the other officer and they confer. I covertly hold Sammy's hand for comfort. When the officer comes back, he tells us to get out of the car.

Sammy and I look at each other. We must do what they say. If we disobey them, the consequences could be bad. We get out of the car, and the officer tells us to follow him to the office.

Bismillah. I am alone in my bedroom again, contemplating recent events.

"*As-salamu alaykum*," a voice greets me. I look up to see the handsome young man who has changed my world, brought me face to face with my truth. I really didn't believe that this man existed; I thought he was a hallucination, a dream. I want to return his greeting, but my voice fails me. He takes a few steps and sits across from me, a smile on his boyish face. He gazes at me for a long time, then reaches for my hand.

"What's your name?" I ask.

The handsome young man points at my wedding band and says, "You're married." I take the ring off and place it on the table. He then proceeds to unbutton my shirt.

"I'm going to make you happy," he says. Sweat starts to bead on my forehead, and my breath quickens. Suddenly, I'm jolted awake. Looking around, I see that I'm alone, a splotch of semen beside me.

"*Allahu-Akbar ... Allahu-Akbar ...*" The Friday call for prayer comes from a distance, the sheikh's voice echoing in my ears. Each syllable cuts into my impure heart. The sheikh intones that God is the greatest, God is the greatest. We as Muslims must be clean and pure. But not me. I'm the sheikh who has repudiated Islam.

I'm drowning in a river of darkness, struggling to breathe. Where am I? Where is Sammy?

"Hello?" I call out over and over. Finally a voice responds: "Ramy?"

"Sammy? What's going on?" I can't see him, can't move. I'm tied to something and my eyes are blindfolded.

"Where are we?" I ask.

"I don't know."

"Help! Help!" I shout. But the only sound I hear is laughter in the distance.

Bismillah. I go into Jaffar's bedroom and see him reading the Qur'an. "What are you doing?" I ask.

"You can see what I'm doing, Baba. You know I do it every evening."

"Don't," I command.

He looks up in surprise. "Why not? I don't understand."

"Where is this book going to take us? We think we know what it represents, but we don't. There are too many lies, *ebny.* Lies."

"But you told me to read the Qur'an every night." He looks confused.

"I made a mistake. We are human beings. We are not infallible. Now, please, don't read it anymore."

"But it helps me go to sleep when I read a few verses."

I pause. I cannot force Jaffar to do what he doesn't want to do. I let him be and leave the room. As I'm going down the stairs, the doorbell rings. It is Ramy's brother, Mohammed.

"*As-salamu alaykum*, brother," he says.

"What are you doing here, Mohammed?" I ask. I feel like returning salaams isn't appropriate anymore. It would be hypocritical.

"It's about Ramy, brother."

"What has happened?"

"He hasn't come home since yesterday, and I'm worried."

Someone takes my blindfold off; the light is dim. My wrists are chained to a wall. Sammy is across from me, chained too.

"What's going on, Sammy?" I whisper.

"I don't know."

His forehead is wet with sweat. I wish I could wipe it away and kiss his brow. As I'm tugging at the chains, trying to free my wrists, the two officers come toward us. They are laughing.

"So what you *lotees* doing here?"

"We're not *lotees*," Sammy replies.

One of them slaps Sammy across the face. I cringe and yell, "No!"

"No?" he says, and slaps me twice. I can bear my own pain, but not Sammy's.

"What have we done wrong?" Sammy asks.

"Your problem is that you're *lotees*."

"No, we're not," I say.

"Are you sure? Let's find out."

They unchain Sammy and turn him around.

"No, no, please!" I yell.

Ignoring me, they unbutton his jeans. I close my eyes. When I open them again, one officer is ripping Sammy's underwear off as the other pulls down his pants and forces himself inside Sammy.

I want to die here and now. Eyes closed again, I listen to Sammy's cries of pain. It's unbearable. I struggle against my chains but cannot get away.

Sammy is whimpering now.

"Please let him go!" I say, knowing how helpless I am.

The officer moans, pauses a moment, then pulls out, dripping semen on Sammy's back.

"Fuck you! Fuck you all!" I scream in rage and frustration.

The officers then turn their attention to me, punching and kicking until I no longer feel any pain. It seems to go on forever.

While Shams is cooking dinner in the kitchen, I am back in my bedroom, after having reassured Mohammed that Ramy would return home safely. I am staring at myself in the mirror when Gabriel appears again, fluttering near the ceiling.

"What have you done to anger Abaddon?" he asks me.

"I took your advice."

"Oh? And what was that?"

"To be true to myself. Now come down here." I reach my arm out to him. Gabriel alights on it, and I hold him tight, kissing him gently on the lips. When I open my eyes, he has transformed into the same handsome young man who visited me before. I turn around, and he kisses my back as he enters me. I feel as if I'm being born. He gives me everything that I need, and I feel complete.

The officers leave our cell. I hope they burn in hell for all eternity. I look at Sammy. He turns away, broken. Through my tears, I say, "Sammy, it's okay, it's okay," but I know it isn't.

They say that everyone in the world is free to love whomever they want. But I tell these people to read my history—and no, I don't want them to cry for me. I tell you that, in Iraq, love is a lie, muddled by religion and tradition and custom.

Do Mohammed and Noor believe that I'm in love with Jameela? Will that keep them happy? I have no love for her. Many Iraqi men have to live with such lies. I'm not the first nor will I be the last homosexual in Iraq.

True love will fight everything that stands in its way. Although my love for Sammy has been put to a test, and he once turned against me, I will never give up on him. I will fight to the very end. I raise my arms and pray to God: You created the world in seven days, but it took me all my life to ask you this, You, whom I believe in no matter what; You, who created those who made me; You, who give life and take it away, I have one question to ask: Why is it wrong to fall in love with a man?

God, I am your creation and yours alone. Since the day I was born, I knew I was not the Iraqi that everyone else tries to be. I am a homosexual, and I can't change that. God, my love for You is strong, but everyone has stood against me. I know You love me and love everyone like me, despite what they say. Please help me and Sammy. Please give us light. Please let us be free.

Bismillah Al Rahman Al Raheem. I am seated again at my wife's dressing table. I pick up the pink lipstick she surprised me with not long ago and smear some onto my lips, admiring myself in the mirror. But then I hear the call for prayer from a distance: *"Allahu-Akbar … Allahu-Akbar."* I am the sheikh in pink.

I look at Sammy again. He turns to face me, and I see the streaks of tears running down his face. I want to see his smile. I want to hold his hand.

"Sammy," I say. "Talk to me."

He continues to weep silently.

Suddenly the door bursts open and the two officers enter again.

"Lotees!" they yell. *"Lotees!"* The word echoes in my ears. They unchain Sammy and pull him away.

"Wait! Wait! Where you taking him? Please, come back! Come back! Sammy!" But no one is listening.

Mino hatha al helw? Who is this person? As I continue to stare at myself in the mirror, I have a revelation. I go toward my night table and retrieve the trimmer that I sometimes use. I turn it on and begin to remove all my facial hair. I am about halfway done when Shams knocks on the door. "Ammar, why is the door locked?" she asks.

"I need some time alone here," I say. "Can you please come back later?"

When I hear her walk away, I continue to shave.

I sit in the darkness, crying, praying for Sammy. Images of his debasement haunt me. The cell door opens, and one of the officers walks in. He places a large tray covered with a cloth on the floor.

I'm not hungry. "Where is Sammy?" I plead. He leaves without a reply.

I look up at the ceiling; Gabriel is fluttering in a corner. "Where is Sammy?" I beseech him.

He doesn't answer either.

When I'm done, I look at myself in the mirror again. Bare-faced with a slash of pink across my lips. Abaddon appears, and I smile at her. "Look at me," I taunt.

She spits at me. "You're disgusting," she says. "You are going to burn in Hell. You deserted Allah and your family for this?"

"I was living a lie," I say. "I just didn't know it."

I keep calling out for Sammy, but no one hears. My stomach is churning. Perhaps if I eat something? I remove the cloth from the tray. I recoil in horror when I see Sammy's bloody head. "*Allahu Akbar, Allahu Akbar,*" I scream but cannot hear myself.

I grab the cloth and throw it back over the tray. I have lost everything. First Ali, and now Sammy. How can I fight this, how can I ever go home?

The cell door opens, and the officers come in. "We're letting you go," one says as he stands over me menacingly. "If you tell anyone about this, we'll hunt you down and kill you."

"No, kill me now!" I beg. "Do it! Just get it over with."

"That's too easy," he says, laughing.

"But why did you kill Sammy?"

The other officer laughs. "Why not?"

Then they blindfold me, drag me out of the cell, and toss me into the back seat of a car. After what seems like an hour of driving, they throw me out onto the side of the road. I try to wriggle around to remove the blindfold, but my hands are tied behind my back. It's impossible.

After what feels like hours, I hear footsteps approach. "Son, are you all right?" a voice says.

"Help me," I say. "Please, help me."

Within moments, my hands are free and the blindfold removed. I thank him over and over. But when he asks me what happened, I turn around and walk away. I cannot say the words. Instead, I look up and stare at the majestic, immortal moon.

Yet another knock at the door disturbs me. Shams says, "Ammar, that young man is here to see you. I think you should come quickly."

In the living room, Shams looks surprised when she sees that I have shaved. Jaffar stares silently at me. I look away from them and am shocked when I see Ramy, who is seated on the couch, bruised and bloodied.

"Ramy, what happened?"

"I'll do whatever they want me to do," he says forlornly. "I'll marry Jameela. I'll do anything."

"But tell me what happened to you!" I turn to Shams and Jaffar. "Please leave us alone," I implore. When they are gone, I sit down and put my arm around Ramy. "I can see that something terrible has happened. This is no time to make rash decisions."

"But I must marry Jameela. There's nothing else left."

I realize he's probably right. I have lived my life as a lie and, as much as I'd like to, I can see no other choice for him. "Surely there's something ..."

"No. I will marry Jameela and try to be happy." He starts to sob uncontrollably. I try to comfort him, but it's no use.

I stand in the kitchen doorway, aware that I haven't cleaned the blood from my face. Mohammed is helping Noor cook dinner. She gasps when she sees me.

"Ramy! What happened to you?" she says. Mohammed stares at me; he doesn't ask any questions. He comes toward me and embraces me. I feel the dampness of his tears on my cheek. The hurt begins to dissipate.

A week later, I find out that somehow, miraculously, I've passed my mathematics exam. Even though it is against my wishes, soon I graduate and receive my degree. During the ceremony, we hear an enormous thudding sound from somewhere in the distance. A building a few blocks away has been bombed. Who knows who is to blame. Just living, just going about our everyday business, is like playing Russian roulette here. Today, death has chosen someone else, not me.

The day I have dreaded has arrived. The sounds of happy voices and music are all around me. People are clapping and laughing. It is a wonderful day for Mohammed and Noor, for Jameela's parents.

As people dance, celebrating our wedding, I am seated next to my bride, feeling numb. Mohammed approaches me. "Can I have a word with you in private?" he asks. I nod and excuse myself from Jameela.

Once alone, Mohammed puts his arm around me. "I just want to say how happy I am now that you're finally married. I promised our father that I would see this happen, and now I've kept my promise. I'm sure you'll make a fine husband and a great father. I'm sure of that, Ramy." He has a contented grin on his face.

"Do you love me, Mohammed?" I ask.

"Of course I do."

"I've always wondered what other promises you made to our father," I say.

Mohammed's smile disappears. "Better get back to your wife," he says.

After the wedding celebrations have ended, Jameela and I depart. We have a hotel room for the night. I sit on the bed, across from her; she is still in her wedding dress. She waits for me to say something, but I cannot speak. Finally she stands up and turns her back to me.

"Can you unzip my dress?" she asks, but still I am speechless. She turns and asks, "What's wrong?"

"Sorry," I reply, then get up and unzip her dress. She lets it drop to the floor and kicks it aside. I look away as she unhooks her bra. I excuse myself and go to the washroom. Taking a deep breath, I try to calm my nervousness. I am trapped ... I don't want to be here. Oh god, what can I do? Looking up, I see Gabriel fluttering near the ceiling.

"Is this what you want?" he asks.

I close my eyes and Sammy appears before me. Unzipping and pulling down my pants, I hold my penis in my hand and begin to pump it. I'm just about to cum when Jameela startles me with a knock on the door.

"Ramy, are you okay?" I unlock the door. "What's going on?"

"I'm sorry. The anticipation ... It just happened."

"Oh."

"I'm very sorry."

She walks away and I quickly tidy myself up and follow her. "I don't ... want to hurt you, Jameela," I say.

"Ramy, it's a work in progress," she says as she puts on her nightgown. She gets into bed and turns her back to me.

I sit down in a chair nearby, thinking about what just happened. I wake up early in the morning, only to realize I had fallen asleep on the chair. Jameela is sleeping peacefully. I hesitate, then undress and crawl beneath the blankets next to her.

Gabriel has returned to visit. He descends from the ceiling, transforming again into the handsome man of Lot. We both know the routine well by now. I disrobe and lay down on the bed and the young man joins me. Many blissful minutes later, he transforms back to Gabriel.

"I'm proud of you," he says, then disappears.

At the dressing table, I trim new hairs from my freshly shorn face and pick up the tube of pink lipstick and trace it carefully onto my lips. I then smudge some on my cheeks and blend it in. Now, looking at myself in the mirror, I am perfect. I am *malikat jamal Iraq*. Inevitably, there is a knock at the door, interrupting my fantasy.

"Ramy is here to see you again," my wife says.

"Tell him to come up here."

Shams says quietly through the door, "Please, not in our room, Ammar."

"It's fine. Let him come up," I say as I continue to admire myself in the mirror.

At the foot of the stairs, I stare at the religious images on the walls; they seem to be mocking me. I am drawn to a family photo of the sheikh dressed in the traditional white gown, the *dishdasha* of an Islamic holy man. His son Jaffar stands between him and his wife, who is covered head to toe in a burka. Only her eyes and hands are visible.

I turn around and face the sheikh's wife. "He will see you upstairs," she says, her voice sullen. As I turn to go up the staircase, she reaches out to my pat my arm, but retreats. A Muslim woman must not touch a man who is not her husband or a close relation.

"Will you please talk some sense into Ammar?" she says.

"What do you mean?" I ask.

"He insists that he has retired from the mosque and refuses to leave our room."

"Oh ... I didn't know. I will try," I tell her.

I open the door for Ramy, and we embrace. "It's been a long time," I say. "You are a married man now."

"Yes," he says. "And you, where have you been?"

"Here," I say, gesturing toward the bedroom. "Where I belong."

I sit on a chair, then notice the smears of pink on his face.

"What's going on?" I ask, not knowing what else to say. "Your wife is worried about you."

"She's always worried." He stands back from the dressing table, looking at his reflection in the mirror.

"How's your wife?" he asks.

"She's pregnant now. We're going to have a son."

He looks directly at me. "You seem happy."

"I am. I've always wanted to have a child."

"Really? You never told me this before." He turns back to the mirror and stares at himself.

"My son ... gives me hope."

"Hope? Look at me. I already have a son, and I'm ..." He stops and turns around to face me. There is nothing I can say to him, nothing I can do for him or for his understandably worried wife.

"Goodbye, Sheikh Ammar," I say as I get up to leave. I pat his shoulder and kiss his cheek. He says, "I take it you're going to name your child after me."

I smile. "No, I'm sorry, I've already chosen the name. It's Sammy."

After Ramy has left, I am alone again with my thoughts. As I look at myself in the mirror, I hear someone call my name. I turn around and see Shams standing before me. Looking at her, I am reminded of our wedding day, when I was able to look into her eyes closely for the first time. I felt calm and at peace. I feel the same now as I look at her radiant gaze.

"Ammar," she whispers. I can see the tears forming in her eyes. She knows my truth.

"Shams, I'm sorry ... so sorry," I say.

I pull her into my arms as I recall Allah's promise for those that will be rewarded Paradise: "And they will be given to drink a cup of wine whose mixture is of ginger from a fountain within Paradise named Salsabeel. There will circulate among them young boys made eternal. When you see them, you would think them as beautiful as scattered pearls. And when you look there in Paradise, you will see pleasure and great dominion."

"God Almighty has spoken the truth."

Acknowledgments

The author would like to thank the following: First and foremost, God, for always supporting and pointing me in the right direction. I want to thank my family: Baba, Mama, Rand, and Mays, for their unconditional love and support. I'm very lucky to have an amazing family whom I love so much. I also want to thank my dear friend Hasheem Hakeem, who has been supportive from the very beginning. I want to thank my friends, my chosen family, whom I love and appreciate. Writers, no matter how big or small they are, are always affected by other writers and artists in one way or another. I'm no different. So many people have inspired me throughout my journey. I have been especially influenced by the stories of the oppressed and silenced. It's the voices of these people who inspired me to write *God in Pink*. I hope that the people in my home country, Iraq, see a better future and that someday everyone will be accepted, no matter what their religion, colour, or sexuality.

In the past few years, major changes have taken place in my life, in which I lost so much. At the same time, I gained much too. I am thankful for all the love and support, and I hope that one day I will be fully accepted by the people whom I love dearly. I want to thank my writing teachers, Jordan Scott and Jacqueline Turner, who have helped me with my novel. I also want to thank all my classmates in my creative writing classes at Simon Fraser University for helping me workshop my novel.

I want to sincerely thank Brian Lam for agreeing to publish my novel and shedding light on the topic. I also want to thank Brian, Susan Safyan, and Linda Field, my amazing editors, for helping me throughout the editorial process. Also, thanks to all the wonderful staff of Arsenal Pulp Press—Gerilee McBride, Cynara Geissler, and Robert Ballantyne—for everything that they have done for me and for the novel.

And finally, this novel is for my "Sammy," Tarnpal Singh Khare, the love of my life. My soulmate. *Ahibak hayati.*

Hasan Namir was born in Iraq in 1987 and came to Canada at a young age. He graduated from Simon Fraser University with a BA in English. He lives in Vancouver.